MW00884704

KING MONTE: THE LOST TIGER'S EYE

MICHAEL A. WOODWARD, JR.

PUBLISHER'S NOTE

First paperback edition in this format 2021.

Summary: Monte Driarson, a bright African American boy, struggles to fit into his school's honors program while maintaining his friendships with students outside the program.

Paperback ISBN: 9798505169650

Hardcover ISBN: 9781087956336

Edited by Emily Fuggetta. Cover design by Sonja Oldenburg. Interior Illustrations by Ekaterina Kuznetsova.

❀ Created with Vellum

For the 29 children in Atlanta, Georgia, who were ripped from the world between 1979 and 1981.

Your spirits live on.

PROLOGUE

INSEPARABLE COULD BE the word used to describe the newfound love Gus had for Monte's Tiger's Eye. Truth be told, it was warm from the way it lay in between the folds of Gus's palms. It was also sticky with the melted ice cream—purchased with stolen food tickets—that oozed through his fingers from the waffle cone that was nearly gone. He wondered if Mrs. Hart-Moore had noticed the tickets were missing but soon became distracted as he spent them on food, food truck after food truck. He had only put the quartz crystal down to eat, yet the moment he was finished, like treasure, back into his pocket was where the Tiger's Eye was buried.

I'm never giving this back to Monte; you're mine forever!

Gus held the Tiger's Eye close to him and kissed it for good luck. Tasting the dairy remnants on the gemstone, he inched forward in line and licked it in an attempt to clean the quartz and relive the sweet treat he had just devoured.

The fuzzy white polar bear that he had just won at the whack-a-mole booth, against himself, had chocolate ice cream on its coat, too. Chocolate streaks smeared as Gus attempted to adjust the bear under his moist armpits while tending to each finger, lifting any bit of ice cream that remained.

"One ticket for the hayride," Gus said in a low voice, head bowed.

The janitor working the ticket booth squinted and put his ear closer to the glass window with holes in it and said, "What? Speak up, son."

"One ticket for the hayride."

The janitor's face sank with displeasure at Gus. "Big boy, I can't help you if I can't hear you!"

Gus's palms began to grow sweaty. His knees began to buckle a little bit. He put a hand in his pocket to find refuge in Monte's Tiger's Eye.

"Yo, Gus the Bus! Hurry up and buy your ticket or get out of line," yelled one of his fifth-grade classmates.

Gus began to breathe heavier as his eyes widened with fear from the attention. His lungs neither inflated nor deflated as he inhaled from his stomach.

"Yeah!" another fifth-grader yelled from the back of the line. "It's not like you're going to be able to fit on the wagon anyway!"

The surrounding kids began to laugh, and even a few parents—dads especially.

Gus's neck vanished as he jabbed his chin into his chest cavity.

A roar of laughter swept behind Gus as he stood there, shoulders drooping, still holding out a fistful of sticky carnival tickets. Even the janitor could be seen grinning through the smudged fingerprints of the plexiglass.

With his opposing hand, Gus let go of the quartz and reached out for the hayride ticket in exchange for the carnival tickets, also stolen from the school counselor.

Just then, Brandon and Jeff could be seen walking side by side. Even with a bandaged nose, Brandon still found the strength to throw salt on Gus's wounds. He saw what was unfolding at the ticket booth and didn't hesitate to elbow Jeff to jump in on the verbal beatdown.

"I knowwwww, you're not thinking of getting on the hayride!?" Brandon said.

Gus's eyebrows began to take the shape of the roofs of houses that lined the Northside neighborhood. He was a master at not crying in public, but behind closed doors he was in no control of his emotions. His bedroom walls were riddled with holes from temper tantrums, and his grandmother usually cried alongside him until they both fell asleep at night.

Gus looked down at his scarred knuckles.

He stayed silent with his head hung as the children went on and on. He tried to make a beeline towards the funnel cake booth in the distance but was cut off by Jeff.

"Where do you think you're going, big boy?"

"He's probably going to get a napkin to wipe the ice cream from his face," Brandon added.

Gus wiped his mouth with his forearm as he saw Monte from afar at the dunk tank with Bao and the twins. Darren, red with anger, was going back and forth with the joke-telling jester. He could see Monte's attempt at sticking up for his friend as they began to argue.

I wish someone would come and stick up for me like that, Gus thought.

He reached for the Tiger's Eye and glared at the fourth- and fifth-graders with the same look of fury and intensity as Monte wore. His scowl and his eyes were a dare to anyone watching as he raised his broad shoulders like a falcon perched high above its prey; the sleeves of his stained black hoodie were beginning to rise just high enough to reveal the scars on Gus's wrists and arms. His eyes turned bloodshot red, and all of the rage that had built up over the years of bullying began to show signs of boiling over. He took a deep breath, and as he bit his bottom lip, he gathered the courage to look his bullies in the eyes and, for once, stand up for himself.

Taking note of Gus's proportions—he was the size of a high-school offensive lineman—they all looked at one another and took a step back in respect of the clear height and weight difference between them.

Gus took a breath like a wind turbine as his eyes began to bulge. His blood began to pulsate through his temporal veins, throbbing as his heart raced. He had never felt like this and allowed it to show. On the outside Gus appeared to be angry and full of rage, but deep down he was afraid.

Brandon began to cower as he adjusted the patchwork on his nose while attempting to hide the blood spatters on his shirt with a buttoned-up jacket.

The fifth-graders, however, weren't as easily fooled.

"He's not gonna do anything, y'all!" one of them shouted. "He's what my uncle calls a gentle giant."

"A big ol' softy!"

"A mama's boy!"

The hot air in Gus's balloon deflated just as quickly as it had filled. His confidence went out of the window and so had the fear in the surrounding fifth-graders.

One of them pushed Gus from behind, causing him to fall down.

"Whoooaaaaaa!!!!!" the children chorused. "Earrthhhquuaakkkeeee!!!!"

The laughter became overwhelming as Gus sought comfort in someone. Anyone. He rolled over onto his back as he scanned the crowd for someone to reach out a helping hand.

Yet all of the hands that were in arm's reach were just fingers pointed at him in a sea of laughter.

Gus pulled Monte's Tiger's Eye from his pocket and shifted his weight from one knee to the other as he slowly rose from the ground. Nearly encircled by his attackers, he found a narrow running lane in between two kids and darted off, leaving his chocolate-stained polar bear behind.

With a baseball in his hand, Monte was elbowed by Darren, who was pointing to where they could see kids huddled together in laughter.

"What's going on?" Bao turned, squinting and pushing his lime-green glasses up his nose. "What's so funny over there?"

"There he is, Monte!" Darren shouted and turned to Bao. "Monte had us looking all over the Southside for him this afternoon!"

"Looking all over the Southside for who? Gus?" Bao quizzed as Monte cocked back his arm to aim for the dunk tank. "That's why you went back to the corner store after school, huh?"

Another miss.

"He has something of mine, Bao, and I'm going to get it back."

"I see." Bao shook his head as the white and red leather baseball rolled slowly back to Monte's newly dirty basketball sneakers.

"I've been looking for him all day," Monte replied, picking up the ball and throwing another miss. "All roads point to him."

"Ha! Maybe your concerned friend with the four eyes has a better chance at hitting the target, Montellous!" shouted the heckler from the collapsible bench. He was dressed as a jester and challenged carnival-goers to hit the target from twenty feet away.

"Forget this clown, y'all," Monte said, motioning toward the hayride ticket booth. "Someone has something of mine, and I'm going to get it back."

Bao looked at the twins as he picked up on no one knowing exactly who had the quartz, or if it was even stolen at all.

1

YOU'RE NO KING

"King Monte, King Monte
They'll all one day say
King Monte, King Monte
Lead us, inspire us, show us the way
King Monte, King Monte
Be great if you may…"

MONTE'S MOM spoke these words into his ear as she knelt at his bedside. The morning chill seeped through the crack of the window and let out the sounds of the TV as it had been left on from the night before.

"And if you call in now, we'll throw in a pair of goose-feather pillows to go along with your brand-new Egyptian mattress," the excited salesmen from the paid-programming infomercial said. "So wake up to a fresh start as it'll be like rolling off of a cloud and being the King you used to be."

Monte scrunched his bushy bed-rumple eyebrows and rolled over to a different spring within his lumpy mattress. There was an outline of Mark in its unevenness from the years of horizontal torment it had suffered before it was passed down to Monte.

"Boy, I knew you weren't sleeping," Monte's mom said warmly.

"Yeah, huh."

"Stop it." Mrs. Driarson paused, switching her tone. "And what did I tell you about leaving your TV on all night, sir?"

Monte peeked his eyes open.

"I'm not playing with you, Montellous. Fall asleep with that tv on once more and I won't be coming in here to whisper in your ear."

There was an awkward silence as the mood had shifted quickly within the room, but like any loving mother, Monte's moved on with her love as though she hadn't just openly threatened him.

"So..." Mrs. Driarson said while raising her eyebrows. "I was checking the weather for tonight's hayride. Seems like it's going to be a beautiful night to be under the stars with a special someone, dear?"

"I don't know what you're talking about." Monte said, curling his lip in protest

"You know what I'm talking about." Mrs. Driarson replied, elbowing her son in the side repeatedly. "Nathalieee."

Monte sighed deeply as he blushed.

"Ok!" Monte's mom said with a smirk. "Keep playing around and you're going to see another King beat you to your Queen."

Monte rolled his eyes. As Bao would say, there were much bigger animals in the jungle at the moment.

Instead, Monte replied, "Yes, ma'am," and gave pause, testing her to see if she would bring up anything else related to school.

"You get any random phone calls yesterday, by chance?" he asked, squinting at her and checking if she knew of the trouble he had gotten into at school the day before.

"Huh?" Monte's mom said, confused. "Just the same ol' bill collectors and college tuition folks. Why do you ask, baby?"

"Oh, no reason, Ma," Monte laughed off dryly. "No reason at all."

Mrs. Driarson shifted her weight from her knee as she sat back onto her heels and narrowed her eyes.

"Is there something you want to tell me, sir?"

"No, ma'am!" Monte said quickly.

"Uh-huuuh," she replied doubtfully. "Are you certain there's nothing you want to tell me?"

"Yes, ma'am," Monte said, hiding between his sheets. "I'm sure."

"If you get kicked out of that honors program, it's going to be me and you. Do you understand, Montellous?"

Nodding slowly, Monte closed his eyes as his mother kissed his forehead and whispered, "I'm excited for the hayride. It's going to be a starry night and a beautiful time."

Monte smiled as she departed his room.

"You're no true king!" The TV spat out.

Peeking from between his blankets, Monte was uncertain if he had fallen back asleep.

"I said... You are no king!" the mattress salesman repeated.

Monte somewhat began to agree with his imagination as he exhaled, half sleep and half in reflection. *I knew I was tripping yesterday,* he thought as he tugged at his jersey-knit sheets. *I should've just kept my mouth closed and listened to the sub. She was just after me,* Monte continued, still selling the dream to himself.

He scanned the dimly lit room as he peered out from the slit between his sheets. He was nervous and wanted to keep his trouble at school away from his parents until after the hayride, but Monte breathed deeply, convincing himself that he'd simply apologize his way out of this mess when the time came.

"A true *king* doesn't just charm his way out of trouble and blame others for his mistakes—"

Huh?

"A true *king* helps his fellow man, takes accountability, and owns up to the consequences of his actions."

Monte closed his eyes to evade the hard truths of his subconscious.

"You're better than that. I thought you were a *king*? Well, then be a *king*."

2

BIG BROTHER WHO?

THE HALLWAY'S shag carpet was lush like marsh-land trees as Monte dragged his feet one after the other without a care in the world. No longer did he have to race to the bathroom and fight his older brother for a steamy shower or a clean sink free of beard trimmings. He could take his time in the morning knowing that it would always be available and waiting for him and only him.

"Hellooo," Monte howled, knocking at the partially open bathroom door before asking a question he already knew the answer to. "Is anyone in here?"

Smiling, Monte flipped the light switch in an unoc-cupied bathroom that was as though it had been off limits to everyone else but him. What excited Monte even more was no longer having to deal with Mark's morning routine of big brother bullying.

Sometimes, Mark would intentionally leave the hot water running long after he was finished just to leave Monte with ice-cold water—glacier showers were what the brothers called them, and they were part of a long list of routine tortures they would perform on one another. But that was no more now that Mark was off at school *enjoying college life* as he would often say on his postcards to Monte.

One by one, Monte had Scotch-taped his postcards to the bathroom mirror, defeating the purpose of being alone and, in a small way, keeping Mark's presence around.

Mornings were calmer and certainly less stressful, and Monte savored every moment of this one as he turned the lever, releasing the hot water in a shower of peace and quiet.

3

JUST THE THREE OF US

"ANY MAIL FOR ME LATELY?" Monte asked, closing the stainless steel refrigerator door.

"I've got some bills for you over here, if you want?" his father quipped.

Monte rolled his eyes at his father, knowing he knew that wasn't what he was referring to.

"I'm talking about from Mark. He said he sent a postcard a few days ago, and it should be here by now, right?"

Monte's father raised and lowered his shoulders in one motion.

Family time was a little different these days as Mark was rarely around. Sometimes Monte sat in his chair at breakfast and dinner to switch things up and bring a little comedic relief in his absence. Sometimes it worked in his favor in getting what he wanted, and sometimes it worked against him and only made matters worse.

"Dad, can I get twenty bucks?" Monte said hopefully, sounding strikingly similar to Mark.

Without lowering his morning newspaper, Mr. Driarson responded dryly, "I thought we got rid of your older brother, King?"

"Dear!" retorted Mrs. Driarson. "Don't talk about my firstborn like that. I miss him so much."

Monte reached out his hand and placed it onto his mother's near the place setting. "It's ok, Mom, I miss him, too."

A tear formed in one of the wells of Mrs. Driarson's eyes.

"Here we go again," Monte's dad sighed as he turned to the finance and investments section of the newspaper. "Go get your mother a tissue, King."

"I'm ok, guys," she said, pulling herself together. "I just miss my baby."

While shaking his head, Mr. Driarson rolled his eyes and replied, "That's a grown man, dear. Let him go."

"No!" she squealed. "Don't say that! He's all the way across town all by himself. All alone."

"Mom, take it easy." Monte smiled, raising his glass of pulp-free orange juice to his lips. "Besides, he told me a few days ago that he might come to the hayride tonight."

"Oh, is that tonight?" Monte's father asked as though he had forgotten while adjusting his reading glasses. "Now, I'm not the biggest fan of wooden wagons being pulled through the neighborhood by horses, but I must admit I do like that event."

Mrs. Driarson gathered herself as she went along with Monte, smoothly changing the conversation to a much lighter topic. "Are you planning on asking your little crush, Nathalie, on the hayride?"

As Monte cleared his throat, his orange juice nearly went down the wrong pipes.

"Are you talking about that cute little freckle-faced girl from the Northside, dear? I remember her, she was at your birthday party over the summer, right?" Mr. Driarson asked, knowing the answer to his line of questioning.

Monte sank deeper into Mark's seat at the table.

"Dear, stop it!" Mrs. Driarson demanded while shooing her husband with the napkin from her lap. "Don't treat my baby and his feelings like that!"

Winking, Mr. Driarson blew a kiss at his son and raised his morning paper back above his eyes. "So. How's school, Montellous? I haven't seen any grades lately."

Monte's eyes widened as he searched for the words, hoping to find them floating in his glass of pasteurized orange juice.

"The grading period isn't over, Pops. And when it is, you'll be the first to know what they look like—I promise," Monte managed with false confidence.

"Well, what about behavior?" Mr. Driarson rallied, returning Monte's serve of hidden truths. "I want to see what those grades look like, as well."

"They don't give grades for behavior, Dad. Duh."

Mr. Driarson folded his morning paper and placed it on the table. He paused and gave Monte the opportunity to realize what he had just said to his father. Moving aside his plate of buttered multigrain toast, Mr. Driarson leaned in closer and remained eerily silent. He interlocked his fingers as he gathered his words and looked directly into his son's eyes.

"I didn't ask you what the markings were for behavior, Montellous. But I'll tell you this, if those conduct grades don't match the academic success I expect to see out of you, it's going to be me and you. Do I make myself clear?"

Monte swirled the remnants of juice around in his cup as he broke eye contact in fear. His mother looked at him from across the breakfast table, fighting to hold back from coming to her son's rescue. She moved her hand back to his underneath the table to provide comfort.

"Yes, sir," Monte said, searching again for those half-truths at the bottom of his glass and praying his dad wouldn't find out about school. "I understand."

"Good," replied Mr. Driarson as he reached into his pocket for lunch money to give to his son.

"Remember, you've always got a choice in life, Montellous. You control your own destiny and choose to be the king we already see you as, so choose wisely."

"I will, Pops," Monte said, assuring his father.

"Fantastic. Now, shouldn't you be getting up out of here and heading to Three Pyramids?"

"Yes, sir. But before I do." Monte paused to find the right words. "Can I get a little extra money to buy two hayride tickets for tonight?"

"I'm not paying for Bao and your other bucket-head friends from the neighborhood—don't they have parents?" Mr. Driarson gibed, pulling back a fistful of folded bills.

"Dear!" Mrs. Driarson said, this time coming to Monte's defense. "Give the boy some carnival money to have a good time."

"I like to have good times, too," Mr. Driarson jeered.

Raising his chin, Monte scratched at an itch just below his neck that wasn't there and muttered, "The other ticket isn't for anyone who lives in this neighborhood."

Monte's parents' eyes met as they exchanged up and down eyebrows.

"Ohhh," his father said while slowly raising his hot cup of ginger tea. "Tell us more, son? We want to know all the deets."

Monte cringed as the word *deets* spilled from his father's mouth in an attempt to sound hip.

Swatting at her husband with the folded newspaper, Mrs. Driarson interrupted the interrogation and ended the questioning. "No need, dear. Give the boy some money and let him be on his way to school."

Cutting his eyes in defeat, Mr. Driarson signaled to his son to lean in opposite from his mother and whispered as he slipped two crisp twenty-dollar bills into Monte's palms, "She can't save you from me every time, son. Remember that."

Monte gulped and sat frozen in fear until his mom squeezed his hand, breaking the trance.

"I've gotta go, you guys," Monte choked out while slinging his backpack over one of his shoulders. "Thanks for the talk."

"We'll be seeing you, King! Make the right choices— or else."

"Hush, dear," Mrs. Driarson said, taking another swipe at the sleeve of her husband's creased dress shirt, "and stop talking like that about our angelic baby boy. All he knows is how to make the right choices—right, Monte?"

"I'm allowed to make a few wrong choices, right—"

"Run, child!" Mrs. Driarson shouted, pretending to hold her husband back from across the kitchen table.

Breaking for the door, Monte snatched his house key from the kitchen counter and shouted back, laughing, "I'm just playing, Pops! I'm just playing."

4

THE TIGER'S EYE

ALL THAT WAS MISSING WAS a bench as Monte stood under the stop sign waiting for Bao as though he was the 7 a.m. city bus.

Dogs barked hysterically a few streets over that Monte could hear alongside the panting of a small purse-size dog at his feet. The Yorkshire terrier didn't seem to be a stray, more likely a recent escapee. Her coat was silky white, and she couldn't have weighed more than seven pounds. A bow was attached to her baby-blue collar that read Jessica, signaling that she certainly did not belong on the streets with the other dogs that typically roamed about.

Jessica? he thought to himself. *What a weird name for a dog.*

Monte looked over his shoulder just to be sure a much bigger dog wasn't creeping up behind him. While Monte wasn't afraid of dogs, he had been bitten by one as a young child, and the traumatic experience had stuck with him over the years.

Visions of Mr. Willow's recently pregnant Rottweiler gnawing at the toes of his new crisp white sneakers still haunted him to this day, along with the trouble he had gotten into that evening when he had to confess to his parents why his brand-new school shoes wore a mother's bite—leaving out the part of him fence-hopping between their neighbors' backyards.

But amidst such an eventful day, there was a different type of music to face today, and Monte knew it. A cringey feeling had lingered all evening last night and much of the morning, spoiling the headline for the day: the fall hayride.

Across the street, a breeze blew orange and brown leaves on the sidewalk at the feet of Bao. He was speed-walking towards Monte while looking at his watch, knowing he was about to hear it.

"Hey, guy, last night you said seven fifteen, right?" Bao smirked, remembering exactly what time Monte had said to meet to make the walk together to school.

Monte looked at his watch, too, and shook his head; he wasn't really in a joking mood this morning, and it oozed through his body language.

"I've got something I want to show you!" Bao told his friend.

Monte shrugged and put his hands into his jean jacket pockets.

"You ok, bro? Seems like you're having a rough morning."

"Me? Yeah, I'm good. Why?" Monte said in a single breath.

Bao laughed. "Oh, I know... You're scared from yesterday, huh?"

Monte shrugged again and withdrew his hands from his pockets to tug at the straps of his backpack.

"Man, I'm not worried about that. I did my work and kept my mouth shut. That sub just didn't like me, that's all."

Bao rolled his eyes.

"For real! You saw how she was singling me out as I was doing my own thing."

"Doing your own thing during independent reading by not reading?" Bao repeated out loud to ensure he was on the same page as his best friend.

"I'm innocent, I tell you."

"You don't have to sell it to me," Bao said as he shook his head in shame. "I told you to chill, but you didn't want to listen. Clearly, that sub was old-fashioned and came with a lot of rules."

"And you know how I feel about rules!" Monte cut in.

The boys shared a quick morning laugh at Monte's stubbornness as the dogs started barking again.

"Why were you over here playing with a dog? I thought you hated dogs?"

"Man, I thought you had something to show me," Monte said, quickly changing the topic. "Hurry up before Big Luther breaks his chain and chases us to school."

Bao looked over his shoulder—Monte's joke only heightened Bao's anxiety of the neighborhood predator. Reaching deep into his pocket, past his bulky eyeglass case, Bao collected an assortment of items.

Monte stretched his neck out as his friend pulled them out, careful not to drop any.

Smirking, Bao looked back up at Monte with his hand closed, hiding its contents. "I've got something for you, bro."

"Well?!" he said impatiently.

Keeping them hidden, Bao paused and drew out the suspense. He peered at Monte through his lime-green prescription glasses and shook his hand like he was holding dice. A light rattling sound led Monte to assume that it couldn't be change.

He rolled his eyes, looking up to the telephone wires that connected the posts.

"Ok. Ok," Bao said, grinning and shaking his fist once more. "But before I do, you gotta promise me that you'll take good care of them. They're special to me, and you'd better not lose them like how you lose everything else in life."

Monte nodded his head as he masked his true feelings disagreeing with his best friend's hard truths.

"I'm serious," Bao said, lifting each finger individually to reveal a set of crystal stones spread across his palm. "Behold!"

Monte sucked his teeth. "Bro... What're these rocks?"

"Rocks?" Bao said in disgust as he held them closer to Monte. "Bro, these are quartz crystals. My mom gave them to me as a child when we arrived from Vietnam; she said they were cut from the highest peak in the Indochinese Peninsula — the Fansipan Mountain.

Monte raised his eyes as he picked up on his best friend's love for his home and culture.

"One day you're a hooper, and the next day you're a geologist. I can't keep up with your interests, bro," Monte poked, smiling.

Bao side-eyed Monte as he spread the semi-precious gemstones across his slick pink palm.

"My mom said each of these crystals mean something," he said, pointing with his other hand at the stones. "This pink one is a rose quartz that represents love, and this shiny black one is called an obsidian quartz. It's thought to protect you."

Monte yawned quietly, yet rudely, nonetheless.

Bao looked up from his palm but did not lift his head nor respond outwardly.

"This one's my favorite!" He reached back into his pocket to pull out the most beautiful stone of his entire collection. It was golden and reddish-brown and shone incredibly, Monte noticed.

"It's called a Tiger's Eye and is said to guide your thinking and provide balance to help you make clear, conscious decisions – the right decisions," Bao said pointedly.

The right decisions, Monte thought, hearing his father's voice in his head.

Bao had Monte's attention now.

"I've made some of my greatest decisions with my Tiger's Eye, and I was thinking last night—"

"Bro — can I hold it?!" Monte over-excitedly asked, whipping out his hands from his jean jacket pockets.

"Naaah! You thought they were whack, remember?" Bao teased.

"C'mon, man, I was just playing – for real!"

Bao laughed as he backed away from his best friend

"So yeah, as I was saying… I was on the porch last night drifting away in another one of the *Tales of the Rice Terraces*." Monte rolled his eyes and drooped his head as his friend spoke, "and I was thinking about the choices both of us made in class yesterday, and I wasn't too proud of them, you know?"

Monte didn't respond and looked down at a black piece of gum that must have been stepped on by hundreds, if not thousands, of kids on the sidewalk. Its shape was molded by sneakers and seemed to have stood the test of time.

Monte thought of the loneliness of the piece of gum and how no one was around to scrape it off of the floor as janitors did in the cafeteria at school.

There was a sense of pride that was taken at Three Pyramids that wasn't taken in the Southside neighborhood. He wondered if the sidewalks of the Northside neighborhoods were paved with spat-out gum and crumpled-up old beer cans like his were.

"Helloooo? Earth to Monte," Bao said, snapping his fingers. "Mr. Wood called my mom and told her how disappointed he was in me last night."

"Get outta here! No he didn't! Why didn't you call me?"

"Call?" Bao chuckled. "I was sent to my room and dared to turn on my laptop or pick up the phone."

Monte's stomach dropped as he wondered if his mom had gotten a call. *Did she know?* Monte thought. *Nah, she would have definitely said something earlier this morning when she whispered to wake me up.*

"Your mom whispers to wake you up, bro?"

"Huh?" Monte said, realizing he was guilt-thinking out loud. "Get outta here with that."

"Whatever, bro," Bao laughed it off. "In all seriousness, I want you to have the Tiger's Eye."

Monte stared at the stone his best friend held out for
him with stirred emotions.

"For real," Bao pushed, holding out the gem, "I think
it'll help you out a lot, Monte. Use it in your most
trying times to help you make better choices."

Monte took the Tiger's Eye as he breathed with
regret. He, too, had begun to believe what his best
friend was saying as his eyes found the black gum on
the sidewalk again, only this time they lay next to
the paws of a Rottweiler who stood with fire in his
eyes.

The dog's silky black coat glistened in the morning
sun as its jet-black tail and matching ears pricked at
attention. Instead of a collar, the Rottweiler wore a
steel army dog tag that read Mr. Willow's litter.

"Bao," Monte whispered, backing away slowly while
keeping direct eye contact. "We gotta make a run
for it."

The Rottweiler growled as its nails scraped at the
black gum on the sidewalk.

"I've got an idea," Bao said, reaching for the obsidian stone in hopes of just enough sunlight.

"We gotta go, bro." Monte stretched, tucking the Tiger's Eye deep into his pocket.

While slowly raising the black obsidian stone between his thumb and index finger, Bao was able to catch the attention of the beast and reflect the sunlight off of one of the stone's jagged edges. Immediately, he discarded the stone onto the ground, and the dog followed it like a tennis ball as it ricocheted off of the cement.

"Run!" Monte shouted as Bao stood in a trance-like state, taking one last look at one of his most prized possessions.

5

STICKY BUNS AND STICKY FINGERS

"IS HE STILL CHASING US?!" Bao shouted, picking up his size-twelve shoes one after the other.

"I don't know! Just keep running."

And run is exactly what the boys did, side by side in an attempt to evade the canine in pursuit. Yet as the boys darted past the string of homes on Rover Street, other dogs caught wind of the chase. Seemingly, they all could be seen on their hind legs through the fences barking and begging for freedom, like inmates in prison.

"We just gotta make it to the corner store, bro!"

"My thoughts exactly," replied Bao in between breaths as he noticed a white SUV barreling through the neighborhood toward them.

Monte squinted as he pumped his arms even harder. His eyes met the halogen headlights of the vehicle between strides and nearly stopped in his tracks. Shaking his head in disbelief, he rubbed the sweat from his eyes and looked again.

"Is that who I think it is?" Bao cried out. "Tell me that's not who I think that is!"

Can't be, Monte thought to himself. *Slink.*

"I thought he was supposed to be in teen jail for that break-in attempt he wanted you a part of?"

"Heck if I know," Monte replied. "Maybe he broke out?"

"Maybe he's here to rescue us again?"

"Ha! Yeah right," Monte countered, veering around the corner while making a beeline to the neighborhood corner store. "Not after I told him I'll pass on committing crimes."

The white SUV sped up, dodging the broken glass in the street. A dark figure appeared as the tinted windows rolled down. A voice poured out from behind the tinted windows, "Hey, you two!"

Bao's eyes widened from behind his lime-green glasses. His knees were nearly jabbing his chest as he drove his sneakers into the ground. He turned his head to see if Monte was behind him and if the dog and white SUV were, too.

"Keep running, bro!" shouted Monte as he sped up ahead of his best friend. "Don't stop!"

"Wait, come back!" An old man appeared, waving and shouting out of the window. "I'm just looking for my dog, Jessica?! She's a Yorkie! She escaped this morning as I was taking out the trash."

Only Bao heard the owner's cries as Monte had run faster in fear of their captors. Unfortunately, Jessica didn't hear them either as she had evaded hers, as well.

With his eyes closed, Monte ran harder, leaving Bao further and further behind. He drove his feet into the ground one after the other as rocks pricked at his feet through his thin soles. He felt the nose of his shoes crease with every step and ground his teeth at the thought of the beating they were taking. Still, he ran harder at the thought of Slink pressuring him to make the wrong choices while avoiding being mauled by a dog half as big as Big Luther.

Filling his lungs with air, he was now at top speed.

"Monte, watch out!" bellowed Bao.

Just then, the door to the corner store flung open as Gus stepped into Monte's path with enough sticky buns to feed a first-grade classroom. There was a loud thud as both Monte and Gus fell to the pavement, and sticky buns went flying.

"C'mon, bro!" Monte said as both boys lay on the cracked concrete. "Watch where you're going, man."

Gus didn't respond as something glistened from between the cracks of the sidewalk, catching his eye. Never minding the countless sticky buns and soda bottles that littered the ground, Gus pocketed something far more precious.

"Are you ok?" Bao probed, helping his friend up from the ground.

"I'm fine. Did you see if that was Slink back there, though?"

"Nah, it was some old dude looking for his dog."

"Go figure," Monte said brushing off the grit of the dirt from his backside and readjusting his clothes from the collision. "You save any sticky buns for anyone else to buy, good sir?"

Gus concealed his newfound prized possession deep into his pocket. "I like sticky buns."

Bao scrunched his face and made direct eye contact with Gus, who quickly looked away to the floor to collect his snacks.

"You think that was Big Luther back there?" Monte said, doubtingly, still trying to catch his breath and looking back to the stop sign.

"Not at all," Bao replied, still looking directly at Gus as he folded his arms and waited to see what he would do next. "I think it was some dog named Jessica."

"Jessica?" Monte frowned, clueless of what was happening right in front of him. "Well, I think they were looking for a much smaller dog."

"No clue," Bao said and cleared his throat, watching Gus climb to his feet while shoving sticky buns into his pockets. Yet Gus pretended not to hear the exchange as he began to make his way opposite of Three Pyramids Elementary.

"Yo, you forgot one, school skipper," yelled Monte, cupping the corners of his mouth with both hands.

"You can have it," Gus said, scuttling away in mischief and mumbling under his breath. "It's the least I can do."

6

MARK'S JOURNEY

IT WAS STILL dark in the sealed room that Mark lay sprawled in. Recycled air flowed through it, carrying an unwelcome odor.

What good are windows that can't be opened, thought Mark, desperate for fresh air amidst the smell of band practice that rose from his roommate's side of the room.

It wasn't hard to identify the culprit of the foul odor. It was a stench that grew by the week as Mark's roommate vowed to never wash his band uniform until the end of the football season. The initials *KB Jackson* were embroidered in a beautiful jade green just below the back neckline of the orange jacket, and white fur sat atop both shoulders. Gold treble clefs tattooed both sleeves of the jacket. Emerald green pants matching the embroidered name held their creases as they suspended from the accompanying dry cleaner hanger KB still held onto since last football season's wash. It was a beautiful garment that touted grace and elegance, but it reeked of halftime shows and sweaty bus rides back from out-of-town games. Everything else from the closet was on the floor.

Inside wasn't the only funk spoiling Mark's moment; the smell of body spray and cheap cologne seeped from under the door, calling Marks attention with its noxious perfume.

"My head is killing me." Mark groaned, lifting an eyelid to ensure he was the only one in the room. "Ahh, he's still gone."

The stillness of being alone reminded him of home. Mark didn't mind at all sharing the spotlight with his little brother. He actually enjoyed how the attention had shifted, which allowed Mark to be left alone and get away with a lot more mischief growing up. He and Monte share many similarities, and mischief was chief among them.

Being the firstborn had its perks, however. He got more leeway with his sense of charm, which Monte had quickly picked up on as he soaked up every exchange his older brother had with his friends and their parents.

Monte learned very quickly when — and when not — to pick his battles with his parents by watching Mark's strategy. He learned the art of speaking less and allowing others to empty their arguments completely. More often than not, he'd watch his older brother show complete control of his emotions and respond with merely a head nod and an uninterested, "I understand."

I feel like I closed my eyes for five minutes, Mark thought, scanning the bedsheets with his palms. *Where's my cell?*

Mark enjoyed being by himself; it gave him the opportunity to think about his next moves in life. Mark needed his thoughts. They kept him sane. Regina, his girlfriend, would disagree at times, begging him to be more open with her. Her empty threats of breaking up with Mark echoed loud and clear when, like Monte, Mark would bottle up his emotions while they battled within his mind.

She's going to be so mad at me, Mark pondered, in search of his cell phone, still dragging his hands in an angelic motion as if in the snow. Pushing away the missed calls and texts from Regina in his mind, Mark shifted his eyes from his roommate's empty, unmade bed and glanced over at the mirror that divided the room. Postcards and books on business systems and fixing cars littered the dresser attached. Some were sprawled open with yellow Post-it notes that served as bookmarks in preparation for upcoming midterm examinations, and some had yet to be opened.

7

LATE NIGHTS AT THE TRACK

JUST A FEW HOURS EARLIER, Mark had been startled as he reached for his key to open his dorm room's door when, to his amazement, it opened right before him and KB emerged with his saxophone case in one hand and an apple cinnamon Nutri-Grain bar in another.

"Whoa!" cried Mark, reaching out for the door as it swung open. "Don't knock me out, sax man!"

"Grandest apologies, Daddy-O," KB replied smoothly while taking a bite of his breakfast and hoisting his black leather saxophone case over his shoulder. "Just making my way to sunrise practice for the halftime show on Saturday."

"Dang, I feel like you just got back from sunset practice."

Smirking, KB shrugged.

Mark had a flashback to similar two-a-day practices during his time on the gridiron. The smell of freshly cut grass soaked in recycled water from the pond behind the high school came to him. The sight of the lights that cast down at practice as his father sat behind the fence watching in support and 5 a.m. meetings all came back to him at once. In the same thought, Mark did and did not miss his days of playing football.

"Now that's dedication," Mark scoffed, licking his thumb to lift the bright orange stamp that got him into the races from his wrist.

"It's the reason why we're the greatest band in the land, roommate," KB said, picking the granola from his teeth. He took another bite and chuckled through his wide nose, "Late-night study session, eh?"

Mark yawned. "I've got an open-hood mechanic midterm exam in a few hours I had to get ready for. I needed to clear my head at the track for a bit."

"And driving 120 miles an hour does that for you?"

"C'mon on, Dad," Mark joked. "I've gotta put my skills at tending to cars to the test. I don't just build cars, roommate. I race them, too."

KB laughed it off but was content in his seniority. Although Mark and KB were the same age, KB had been in school for three years and was set to graduate next fall – right after marching band season.

Mark laughed, but KB's medals and section leader status on campus said otherwise. The band at Florida Automotive and Technology University, known as The FATs Domino Band was a serious thing. It seemed much of the city supported the band more than the abysmal amateur sports teams that competed within the city.

Collectible drum major hats and vintage musical instruments sold for thousands of dollars online, and T-shirts lasted minutes on store shelves during marching band season. It was even said that the students and alumni of FATs went to the football games for the band more than they did for their own football team.

Mark began to recount conversations as a child with his parents...

"Mmhmm, I can still hear the soothing sounds of the saxophone solos and the blare of trumpets leading the brass section—"

"And the heartbeat of the drums as they set the tempo for everyone's feet in the stands!"

No longer interested in talking about the band after countless hours of *studying* that evening, Mark pulled out his cell phone and sighed.

I can't believe I stayed out that late, Mark thought as he wormed his way past his roommate and slid his hotrod car keys across the desk he and KB shared.

The keys came to a halt over a postcard Monte had written to him about a bad day he had had earlier that week.

To Big Bro,

Can't believe you're really gone.
Sometimes, I sit in your chair
at dinner and pretend to be
you. It makes Mom and Dad smile
— sometimes. I think it helps
them accept you've really moved on.

Honors classes are honors classes... blah.

Hope to see you at the hayride.

King Monte

Mark Driarson
Florida A&T University
1906 MLK Drive
Old Gold, FL 33029

Mark looked at the postcard and, in that moment, thought more of his bed that awaited him than reading his little brother's heartfelt words.

It was a back and forth type of relationship the brothers shared since Mark's departure for college, but after a late night of prepping for his mechanic midterm later that day and making a couple of extra dollars, reading about Monte's fourth-grade honors-kid problems were the last thing on Mark's mind.

8
_____

ORANGE JUICE

THE SMELL of apple cinnamon pancakes and warm syrup filled the air in the cafeteria as students and families exchanged goodbyes and I love yous. Shades of pink and red lipstick were left imprinted on the faces of children throughout the room. The kindergarteners and first-graders typically wore them proudly, while fourth- and fifth-graders could be seen wiping them off immediately.

While Darren and David made their way to the breakfast they had been looking forward to since the night before, Monte stood in line tugging at the straps of his backpack. Something was off, and he knew it. He checked his pocket for his house key and breathed a sigh a relief. *Thank goodness*, he thought.

Mr. Wood stood motionless at the head of the line with a used tissue clenched in one hand and a sun-kissed orange in the other. His arms were folded and his feet were squared. Usually, he greeted his students with high fives, warm smiles, and head nods. But not this morning. The note from the sub lay folded within his plaid front pocket.

"I told you he was going to be mad," Lizbeth whispered.

Nathalie ground her teeth together, and without opening them she asked, "You think he knows about yesterday?"

"Duh!" whisper-yelled Lizbeth. "Look at that poor orange."

Brandon and Jeff shuffled as they found their places in line along with the rest of the class.

"Still got the Tiger's Eye, right?" Bao murmured from behind in a low whisper.

Monte's stomach dropped as he patted his pockets for the stone. He knew immediately why a feeling of unease trailed after him into the cafeteria.

"Helloo?" Bao probed, suspecting he already knew the answer to his line of questioning.

At first Monte stayed quiet, hoping Mr. Wood would call for order, yet he did not. Instead he stood in a trance-like state, still woozy from the cough syrup he had taken.

"I knew you'd lose it, Monte," Bao said under his breath. "You lose everything, man."

Gus! Monte thought, replaying the morning in his mind. "Of course I still got it," he lied. "I can't believe you would think so low of me, bro."

Bao squinted his eyes and went along to see how far Monte would spin his web.

Mr. Wood saw the girls looking and talking to one another as he loosened his grip on the Florida orange, wiping a bit of the juice on his creased plaid pants.

"Ahh, welcome back Mr. Wood – I hope you're feeling better," Ms. Bleacher shouted, half-genuinely, to her fellow fourth-grade teacher. "Your line sure looks a heck of a lot better than it did yesterday! Your kids were so rowdy, we heard rumbling down the hallway like boulders in a landslide."

The hairs on Mr. Wood's pencil-thin mustache began to rise. His lip began to curl, and Monte thought Mr. Wood was going to explode at Ms. Bleacher. He could see his teacher's chest rise as his lungs inflated with air and eyes widened. Yet as his lips began to form ice-cold words in response to his colleague's attempt at teacher-shaming, his eyes met Monte's, and he dropped his near flattened orange.

"Why thank you, Ms. Bleacher," Mr. Wood replied, bending over to pick up his fruit. "I, too, have caught wind of the poor choices my scholars made yesterday in my absence." He turned his attention back to the silent, sword-straight line that stood before him.

Realizing he was no longer concerned with her opinion, Ms. Bleacher raised her nose and gathered her students to lead them out of the cafeteria.

From across the way, Monte could see the twins making light of their teachers' passive-aggressive confrontation. They were giggling and making faces at the exchange, but Monte wasn't laughing at all. At this moment, he didn't know if he felt bad for Mr. Wood being slightly embarrassed by his colleague or if he felt worse for how he himself had treated the substitute the day before. What he did know was that there certainly wasn't anything funny about either of those scenarios as he half-smiled and nodded at the twins' departure to the B Pod.

"See you at recess, Monte!" shouted David.

Mr. Wood's eyes seemed to shout, too, as they landed on Monte.

He had seen that look a thousand times from both his mother and father. It was a serious and a question-of-certainty face. The kind that makes your eyebrows rise to the top of your head and stand paralyzed, like a deer blinded by headlights on an eerie country road.

Mr. Wood underscored the look he had just given Monte by folding his arms and, somehow, bringing his eyebrows even closer to one another. He gestured to Monte to face forward in line and continued to make eye contact with each of his scholars. He slowly shook his head from left to right as he continued to stand square with his toes pointed outward at the head of the line.

Realizing they were the last class left in the cafeteria, Mr. Wood's students continued to stand in silence as knees began to lock. All of the parents had said their goodbyes and were off to work. There was no one to save them from Mr. Wood. The joy of disrespectful and rowdy behavior from the day before was no more, and as Monte's father used to say to him and his brother, it was time for their chickens to come home to roost.

Mr. Wood's nostrils flared as he paced back and forth.

The janitors had begun to make their way into the cafeteria armed with mops, brooms, and floor scrapers. It was going to be a busy day for them as they were tasked with not only staying until late to clean up after the Hayride Festival but setting up for it, as well.

Pots and pans could be heard being shuffled from the kitchen as the cafeteria workers flipped on some old-school music and began preparing for lunch. The janitors began to electric slide with their brooms and mops in unison. They were working hard, but you couldn't tell by how much fun they were making of it. No one in Mr. Wood's class was dancing as they continued to stand, one directly behind the other in a perfectly straight line. No one was tapping their feet, and certainly no one was singing.

Mr. Wood whistled as he continued to stretch out the uncomfortable moment between him and his students right in the center of the cafeteria.

Monte's eyes wandered from the back of Brandon's brown leather camping knapsack onto the floor again. He noticed the gum that was stuck to the floor near the vending machines and thought of the littered beer cans and gum on the sidewalk earlier on the street. The difference was that, before he knew it, one of the janitors was scraping up the gum at Three Pyramids Elementary. Monte knew that no one was going to make that same effort near his home.

"Monte, goooo," whispered Bao from behind.

Where a gap had begun to form, Mr. Wood stepped in front of Monte and Bao, who were at the very end of the line. With his feet planted, Mr. Wood turned and craned his neck, signaling to his class to continue heading to the stop sign at the corner.

"Good morning, Mr. Wood," the boys said as they both avoided eye-contact with their mentor.

"Don't 'good morning' me, gentlemen. I'm not having a good morning. You heard what Ms. Bleacher said to me a moment ago." He shifted his eyes to Monte.

Monte didn't respond. He wasn't ready for the sudden change of focus from Bao to him at that moment and was a second too late at escaping Mr. Wood's glare. While he was furious on the outside, his deep brown eyes said otherwise as shame and disappointment puddled within them.

"I spoke with your mother last night, Mr. Bulvarian," Mr. Wood said, folding his arms and turning back to Bao.

"I heard, sir."

"She was hurt, too, you know? She told me that a teacher had never called her before to share tough news about you in school," Mr. Wood said, shaking his head and trying to mold his orange back into the sphere-like shape it had been when he'd left his home. "It's my hope that you two bring out the best in one another. You've got to make each other better as friends, you know, not worse."

Monte and Bao glanced at one another to see if Mr. Wood's words had stung with equal intensity. Their shoulders drooped, but Bao picked his chin up and found the pseudo-courage to mumble, "Yes, sir. She came into my room crying, yelling, and throwing things."

Monte was now shaking his head, knowing his mom was going to do way more than cry, yell, and throw things when she heard the news.

"And how'd that make you feel, sir?"

Bao recoiled. He closed his eyes for a moment, seeming to hide behind his glasses.

"And how'd that make you feel, sir?" Mr. Wood repeated.

"It made me feel horrible. I hadn't seen her cry like that since my father left. She just kept saying how disappointed she was in me. It was all bad, sir."

"And how do you think that substitute felt yesterday when you wouldn't stop talking during her instruction?" Mr. Wood inquired, leaning into Bao's personal space but directing his attention to his classmate. "And don't think you're out of the woods just because the Driarson home didn't get a call last night, Montellous."

Monte poked his lip out.

"Who did you think you were telling that lady what you weren't going to do? Did you forget who the teacher was and who the scholar was?"

"No, sir," Monte said shortly.

The whispers of the rest of the class could faintly be heard from the hallway where they were standing, waiting to move forward.

"What's going on, Lizbeth?" whispered Nathalie.

"Yeah, what are they doing?" another kid in line added.

Brandon turned around from the head of the line and butted in, saying, "I hope he's giving it to Monte. He deserves it."

"Shut up, Brandon. You deserve a heck of a lot more than what Monte deserves for being the kind of person you are!"

"What's that supposed to mean, Nathalie?"

"Would you guys be quiet before Dr. Styles comes out of her office!" Lizbeth said, stepping out of line to wag her finger at her classmates. "Besides, they're just standing there while the janitors are dancing in between the lunchroom tables."

"That's my auntie's favorite song," Nathalie said to herself.

"Well, Bao and Monte certainly aren't dancing," replied Lizbeth as she shuffled her feet back in line and stood at attention. "They're coming!"

Mr. Wood's class all scrambled to reform their once perfect line, trundling their feet and kicking the baseboards of the hallway walls in the process.

"Bruhhhhhh," sighed Lizbeth.

Brandon turned around making an ugly face and said, "Chiiill, Liz! Geesh, I bet Dr. Styles isn't even—"

"What's going on out here?!?" The door of Dr. Styles' office swung open, and the students could see a parent and student at a round table past the principal's roaring orange and red earrings. "Why are you all not in class? Where is Mr. Wood?"

Mr. Wood's class stood paralyzed in fear as, yet again, they had found themselves in trouble.

"I'm right here, ma'am," Mr. Wood said as his hard-soled shoes click-clacked their way through the cafeteria doors. "Just holding a few one on ones with the kids as I heard they had quite a day with the substitute yesterday."

"Oh, I heard," Dr. Styles replied, folding her arms and motioning for the hallways to be cleared. "I heard."

9
_____

A SPECIAL GUEST

THE BOYS and girls approached classroom thirty-two, where the door was cracked open.

Breaking their silence, Lizbeth and Nathalie looked at one another and then up at their teacher and quizzed, "Why is your door open, Mr. Wood?"

"Yeah, you never leave your door open."

With his index finger over his mouth, he whispered, "Shh, we have a special guest today."

"A special guest?" another student chimed in.

Mr. Wood rubbed the sides of his head as his sinus headache began to return.

"Good morning, Mr. Wood's fourth-grade honors class."

"Who's that?" Brandon scoffed from the back of the line, stretching his neck to see inside of the classroom.

"Good morning, Ms. Heart-Moore," the class said back in broken unison.

As the founding school counselor, Mrs. Heart-Moore had seen the neighborhood kids clash for years over the decades. She was a pale and oval-ish woman who wore her jet-black wig and hot-pink lipstick proudly in full support of women's rights whether she was in her small groups with students or on the streets marching for equal rights as she had in her youth.

She was considered one of the best at Three Pyramids Elementary and had drawn attention from the masses by earning several district counselor of the year awards. She was famous for her intervention strategies with at-risk youth who were on the edge of making some pretty horrible decisions and garnered the school profitable attention.

Despite all of the fame, however, Mrs. Heart-Moore never left Three Pyramids Elementary and continued to intervene in the reoccurring squabbles between the kids from the Southside and Northside neighborhoods.

"All right, boys and girls. I couldn't be happier to be here with you all. I see some new and familiar faces in the honors program." Mrs. Heart-Moore nodded in warmth and welcome in their direction as she snaked her way through the classroom, stopping and pausing just in front of Monte's desk.

"Well, well, well. I heard the news, and I couldn't be happier for you, Monte – welcome."

Brandon rolled his eyes in the distance as Nathalie did the same, only hers was cheeky and Brandon's was envious.

Monte half-smiled and nodded back, unappreciative of the spotlight. He knew of Mrs. Heart-Moore, however. Over the years, he had seen her making her social-emotional learning session rounds to classes within the B Pod; they were the majority of her one-on-one and group interventions. Her care ran deep for the kids from both neighborhoods.

"I see we've got a new teacher, as well, in the honors program, huh, boys and girls?"

The class giggled as Mr. Wood poked out his lip and scrunched his eyebrows.

"I'm sure he's doing his very best, right?" Mrs. Heart-Moore made a dubious face, as though she didn't know for sure.

They all laughed, some harder than others, including Jeff and Brandon.

"Okay, okay," Mrs. Heart-Moore soothed, "settle down now."

She looked at the clock — she was a stickler for time and took punctuality very personally. She waited for the respect she demanded, however.

"We're glad to see you, Mrs. Heart-Moore," Nathalie spoke out as the class calmed down. "You've been to all of the other fourth-grade classes, but not ours."

"Not cool, Mrs. H," Lizbeth said, slowly shaking her head.

Mrs. Heart-Moore's mouth fell open. "Now, girls!" she pleaded. "Maybe because of the boys I took my time to get here, but for you all I would never."

Mr. Wood chuckled as Mrs. Heart-Moore brought her voice to a whisper. "Honestly, it's because I was saving the best for last."

Nathalie and Lizbeth both smiled with love and adulation.

"Now, class," Mrs. Heart-Moore commanded as she began to set up her lesson, "physically, who thinks they are the strongest in here?"

All of the boys and more than half of the girls in the classroom raised their hands. Some had even gotten out of their seats and began to flex their biceps as though they were competitive bodybuilders.

Mr. Wood's face folded in like an accordion.

Jeff and others immediately returned to their seats.

"I see," Mrs. Heart-Moore replied wide-eyed as she caught the effect of the teacher-stare Mr. Wood had shot at his scholars.

"Now, mentally," she paused for emphasis while writing the word on the dry-erase board, "mentally, who thinks they're the strongest in here?"

Perplexed, no one moved as Mrs. Heart-Moore made eye contact with each student as she dragged her tilting wedge shoes past them, one by one. She raised her pencil-drawn eyebrows to reinforce her questioning as she moved throughout the room, hands tucked behind her back.

Everyone looked at one another in silence.

Brandon smirked and raised his hand but spoke without being called on. "You mean like the smartest in here? Because if we're talking the smartest, then that's gotta be me!"

Everyone now looked at one another in frustration.

Mrs. Heart-Moore shook her head in disappointment as she eyed how her toes slightly hung over her worn-down sandals. Lizbeth saw, too, and put her hand over her mouth.

"So outside of Brandon, no one believes in their mental strength?" quizzed Mrs. Heart-Moore, rocking back and forth.

Mrs. Heart-Moore gave Mr. Wood's students time to process her question.

Seconds passed by, and still no hands went up, all the students uninspired by Brandon.

"Hm," Mrs. Heart-Moore thought out loud, tapping her lips with her index finger. "But I thought we all had muscles a moment ago, boys and girls?"

Monte's hand rose slowly.

"Ahh, Monte?" Mrs. Heart-Moore replied as Nathalie began to glow. "You have a question?"

Monte cleared his throat, realizing there was no turning back.

"Well?" Mrs. Heart-Moore pushed as the cringey feeling began to seep into the lining of his stomach.

"I mean, I don't want to say I'm the strongest in here or anything," Monte said, exhaling while lifting his chin slowly, "but I do think my mind is strong."

Mr. Wood folded his arms and lowered his eyebrows.

"Ahh," Mrs. Heart-Moore said, cracking a smile. "Do tell us more, Mr. Driarson."

Monte sat up in his chair a little taller. He cleared the harshness from his voice to articulate his words. He knew he was in too deep to deny Mrs. Heart-Moore's request. He had already spoken up, and everyone was zeroed in, as usual, on Monte's next words. He basked in the silence and thought carefully of his next ones.

"Sometimes when I think something's too tough or too challenging, I think of my ancestors. I think of the Black kings and queens my mom and dad still tell me about to this day." Monte paused, looking around at his honors classmates. "When I think of giving up, I think of them, and that gives me the mental strength to go on."

Mrs. Heart-Moore turned and looked at Mr. Wood and said in a low whisper, "I told you there was something beautiful in that young man."

10

SHADY 8'S SECRET

THERE WAS a trail of old leaves and even older meat market and deli coupons leading into Building S of the abandoned Shady 8's apartment complex.

It was really Building 5, but to the common eye, it read Building S — a loose, rusted screw caused the 5 to hang and mislead.

Gus never cared what it read; he knew where his hiding spot was in the complex. It was the only building that still had a powerline attached to it near the courts with the tattered volleyball nets.

Gus knew he could ground a loosely connected line and connect it to an old car battery he'd *borrow* from his grandad's garage.

Graffiti riddled the once beautiful paint job of Shady 8's. Beyond the territory markings and teenage expressions of art on the buildings, there was a sense of community that radiated from the barely still-standing structures.

There was a dark and looming yet warm presence – old and new.

Sunset oranges and soothing mocha browns danced from balcony to balcony. The accents of the bronze stairwell railings, antique light fixtures, and copper-colored canopies were no more; the apartment's management and residents had all seemed to vanish overnight.

Missing children flyers hung from rusted nails while many more littered the playground and parking lots throughout the complex. There was a secret within Shady 8's that many spoke of but few truly knew.

Gus dragged his feet over the weathered off-white parking space lines. There wasn't a single car within the complex to fill them.

Sometimes at night a police car parked just outside of the unmanned security post at the entrance of the complex, but the officer usually napped while squatters used other entrances to find a place to sleep at night, so his use wasn't much warranted.

"Hellooo?" Gus said, ensuring he was alone in the hallway. Stepping into the darkness, he reached into his pocket, past his sticky buns, for the black and yellow screwdriver.

Shady 8's – Unit 2B

Chewed-through cables from satellite dishes swayed, disconnected, in the wind.

Porch screens were torn, weeds were growing through the cracked concrete, and the doors of mailbox units all opened and slammed closed free from their popped locks.

Stapled and halfway torn signs that read *Trespassers Will Be Prosecuted* hung from light poles and entrance walls into the apartment complex, yet kids told stories of the shadows cast by slouched figures seen between the gaps of the boarded up windows.

As if that wasn't eerie enough, sometimes the unattended parking lot lights flickered in the night, illuminating the dark entranceways to the abandoned buildings just enough to see hidden figures in the dark.

No longer did middle-class Black families play volleyball near the now-decaying green gazebo constructed beside the algae-ridden pond.

Scorched tire marks that led to the final resting place of countless neighborhood kids who were ripped away from their families still lay in a trail heading away from the playground.

Still, even as danger and death loomed just beyond the broken steel gates of Shady 8's, within the shadows, life was there.

Inside of one of the units, the walls were green with spores of mold and mildew. The drywall that once needed a hammer to nail in support now could easily be punched through.

The air was thick with bacterial particles that could be seen floating freely as the wind made a humming sound through the broken windows.

Without care, Gus plopped down into a recliner he'd recovered from a makeshift dump of discarded tube tvs and old furniture near the mailboxes outside.

Believing everything was for the taking, Gus hadn't thought twice the day he spotted "his" recliner buried beneath a broken baby crib and sagging mattress.

Shifting his weight, Gus pulled the new flathead screwdriver he'd lifted from the cornerstone from his pocket and laid it next to a similar one on the table, only that screwdriver was broken in half from forced entry, as was another at the foot of the front door.

Gus pulled back the lever releasing the foot rest from the recliner.

Using his teeth to gnaw through the plastic covering of his sticky bun, he reached for the latest issue of the *Jarod the Fraud* comic on the end table just left of the armrest.

Jarod the Fraud, whom Gus considered an anti-hero, stole things from others either to keep for himself or share with his closest friends. Gus found a connection with the character who benefited from quick come-ups and stolen goods.

He believed it was okay to cause such mischief and never thought twice of placing himself in the position to win, even if it was at the downfall of others.

Gus leaned back even further in the recliner as he began to drift away, seeing himself in the comic.

11

WHERE THERE'S SMOKE, THERE'S FIRE

THE SOUND of the fire alarm blared throughout the school as children and adults made their way down the hallways. The voices of teachers hurrying their students began to echo, all saying the same things to their students.

"Keep up, keep up; move it along."

"No running!"

"Close the gaps."

Mr. Wood's class navigated their way past the restrooms and onward to the field beyond the recess blacktop. There were kids and teachers everywhere — the exit doors seemed to represent a faraway finish line in a too-long race.

"Let's pick up the pace in the back, fellas."

Monte knew that his teacher was referring to him but didn't pick up his pace, instead continuing on with his conversation with Bao as the chaos surrounded them.

"I'm just glad we got out of math class. It felt like recess and lunch were forever away—"

"Excuse you!" Monte scowled as someone jostled him, and a shrill voice from below said, "I'm sorry, mister."

"Hey! I know you." Bao snapped his fingers, trying to recall the kindergartener's name. "You're in my little sister's class."

Monte cut his eyes at the kid, refusing to accept the apology from the little boy. "Shouldn't you be with your class or something?!"

"I'm Jeremy, and I'm lost."

"A fire drill is the last place you want to be lost, little man," Bao said, bending down on one knee and pointing towards the kindergarten hallway.

"Yeah, so beat it, little Jeremy, before the fire engulfs you," Monte teased with sarcasm.

"Noo!" Jeremy shouted, running off nearly in tears.

"Well, at least he's running in the right direction," Bao said, shaking his head.

"So what, bro? There isn't a real fire, you know," Monte remarked, laughing at Bao's seriousness.

"Gentlemen," Mr. Wood said, standing behind them. He cleared his throat.

"Uh-oh," Bao said with both eyebrows raised. "He said he was lost—"

"Just stop," Mr. Wood said, turning his cheek with a palm raised. "Tell me I didn't just see what I think I saw."

"We were just messin' with him, Mr. Wood," Monte downplayed, looking at Bao.

"He didn't deserve that kind of treatment. We'll talk about it later. Right now, you two need to catch up with the class!"

There was a fierceness in Mr. Wood's voice as he quickly reprimanded his scholars.

"Everyone should be moving out the door!" demanded the school resource officer. "Let's go!"

12

A KING IN QUESTION

OUTSIDE, Dr. Styles stood with her favorite clip-board and a stopwatch counting the passing seconds. There was a fire truck just beyond the rows of classes that outlined the school's field like a marching band missing its musical instruments. Aside from the alarm that still rang, there weren't really any sounds at all. Teachers stood at the heads of their lines with their fingers over their mouths, indicating that this was not the time to talk.

"Right here's good," Mr. Wood said, pointing to an opening between two other fourth-grade classes. "Mouths should be closed, and we need to still be in our line. Where's Nathalie?"

"She's up here in the front, Mr. Wood!"

"I'm right here, and I've got your clipboard!"

"Shhh!" another teacher hissed.

Mr. Wood approached wearing a scowl as though he was ready to single them out for speaking so loudly, but he immediately gave them a warm smile, put his finger over his mouth and took the clipboard from Nathalie.

"Thanks," he whispered while winking at the two of them and backing away to take attendance quietly. "Lizbeth, Brandon, Erin..."

"Psst, yo, Monte!" a voice from another line called out.

"Monteeee."

Bao nudged Monte, who was standing behind him, and hinted to look to where the voices were coming from.

"Huh?" Monte replied, coming back to reality.

"Over here!" the twins whispered loudly.

Looking at the boys through a line of fourth-graders between them, both Monte and Bao made basketball shooting gestures.

"Oh yeah?!" mouthed Darren.

David held up his wrist and pretended to point at a watch that wasn't there.

Monte leaned forward closer to Bao and said, "They couldn't take me before you, and now they definitely can't stop me when we play together."

"I think you mean they can't stop *me*, Monte," Bao retorted, chuckling.

"Get outta here."

"Hey, let me see the Tiger's Eye for a quick second, bro!"

Monte's eyes widened as he searched for an answer in the sky. He thought of taking the road less traveled and telling his best friend the truth, but he also thought of taking the easy way out and simply telling another lie. His stomach churned. He had to think of something quick. Instead, he reached in his pocket as though the stone would magically reappear.

"Gentlemen!" Mr. Wood said sharply. "You're already in hot water with me; are we adding on to your time on the wall now?"

"No, sir," replied Bao with his chin pinned to his chest.

Monte, on the other hand, rolled his eyes and shrugged his shoulders in the direction of Mr. Wood.

"Something you want to say to me, prince?"

Monte paused and appeared broken in that moment as he gathered himself.

"I'm no prince — I'm a king."

Mr. Wood stepped closer, stooping to make direct eye contact with Monte while invading his personal space, and whispered, "I can't tell."

Monte considered talking back but thought of his parents. He had had countless back-and-forths for the last word, usually ending in tears. As such, Monte kept his mouth closed as he surveyed the neighboring fourth-graders, who all nudged one another to observe the bubbling confrontation.

"Yes, sir," Monte replied dryly.

"I expect better from you, Montellous. Yet lately you've been letting me down. You've been coming off as though you're above others, and I don't like it. Where's the lion-hearted king I met back in August?"

Monte scratched at an itch that wasn't there.

Mr. Wood rose slowly as he looked over Monte into Bao's eyes in a way that acknowledged he was beginning to go down the wrong road, as well.

"Do better, gentlemen," Mr. Wood continued in a whisper. Y'all are supposed to be my leaders in the classroom, yet you push the little kids around and set the wrong example for your classmates—"

"But—"

"I don't want to hear it, Montellous," Mr. Wood shouted, jabbing his index finger into Monte's chest. "Tell me about it on the wall during recess!"

Monte and Bao looked at one another in dismay. They knew they weren't the kids Mr. Wood thought they were in that moment, but they also knew that they deserved the shake of every head that surrounded them — including Nathalie's.

13

THIS TIME IS UNACCEPTABLE

THE FINAL MOMENTS of the fire drill were silent. The alarm had been reset from within the building, yet no one moved as they all awaited the signal from Dr. Styles, who stood embarrassed at the abysmal evacuation time her stopwatch read.

"This is unacceptable," she said to her office secretary, Mrs. Sheffield. "Were they strolling out of their classrooms!?"

Mrs. Sheffield shifted her weight onto her other heel on the soft grass. "I don't think the fire chief is going to be happy."

"When is he ever, Mrs. Sheffield?"

Meanwhile, pickup trucks began to outline the perimeter of the P.E. field towing rickety trailers that carried carnival booths and farm animals. The smell of manure flowed through the fences as the entire school stood in disgust. Kids covered their faces and teachers fanned their noses as the sounds of laughter seeped throughout the sea of students.

It was a short moment of ease amid a few long moments of tension.

Yet the firefighters, who had a stopwatch of their own, weren't laughing at all.

"These times are not good enough, Miss Styles," said Fire Chief Chism as he repositioned the axe that swung from his utility belt. "If a fire was to break out, it would be a serious breach of fire code, which would prohibit your students and teachers from exiting safely, ma'am."

Dr. Styles nodded slowly.

"I'm giving you a warning this time," the chief said, holding his index finger up as his rubber boots began to squeak off into the distance. "Enjoy your little hayride, Miss Styles.

"That's Dr. Styles, Chief Chism," Mrs. Sheffield interjected, coming to her principal and best friend's defense. "She earned that title just as you did yours."

Dr. Styles folded her arms as she looked across the field onto her students and teachers, who all stood oblivious to the exchange.

"What're they talking about?" Nathalie said, nudging Lizbeth.

"I don't know, but Dr. Styles looks about as mad as Mr. Wood just was a bit ago."

"Yeah," Nathalie said softly, looking over her shoulder at Monte. "I hope that doesn't stop him from coming to the hayride tonight."

"You just wanna ride on the hayride with him through the neighborhood, huh?"

"Who wouldn't want to lie down and look up at the stars while drifting away to the sounds of the hooves of horses?"

"Stars, huh?" Lizbeth said with a curled lip. "Wait, you can't even lie down in that little ol' wagon."

"Girl, stop being a hater," Nathalie shot back as they began to giggle.

"Take us away, ladies," Mr. Wood said as he pointed to the side of the dull gray- and red-roofed building with his other finger over his mouth.

One by one, the grade levels all marched in single-file lines from their places against the fence that ran parallel to the neighborhood's Main Street.

"Mr. Wood," Dr. Styles called out, flashes of orange and red reflecting from her earrings. "A moment of your time, please?"

Mr. Wood knew that wasn't a question that required a yes or no, and Monte knew that, as well, as he squinted his eyes and put his hands into his jean jacket pockets.

"Think he's about to get in trouble?" Bao whispered.

"Nah, not Mr. Wood. He's like my fast-talking big brother, Mark. Besides, teachers don't get in trouble… Right?"

Bao shrugged his shoulders and flipped his wrist to adjust his digital watch.

"I'm not happy about the conduct your class displayed out here and in the building, Mr. Wood."

"Yes, ma'am."

"You had kids talking and taking their time getting to their positions out here, and that's simply unacceptable."

"I understand, Dr. Styles — we'll be sure to get a bit of practice in to be better prepared for the next fire drill."

"Thank you, sir. And by the way, how is young Montellous doing these days?"

Mr. Wood hesitated, wondering whether to share his growing concerns about one of his favorite scholars, but refused to share his recent disappointment of him in fear of losing him from his class.

"He's well; I grow more proud of him as the days pass us by."

"Beautiful!" remarked Dr. Styles as her earrings softened and began to radiate a deep ocean blue. "You know his family will be here tonight? Have you had the chance to meet them yet?"

"You know, I unfortunately haven't, since open house landed on a bad time for them." He placed his hands in his plaid pockets and shifted his weight. "His mother wrote me in her absence, however. She certainly seems as though she doesn't play around with young Monte."

Dr. Styles chuckled to herself and quickly reminded her fourth-grade teacher of his shortcomings during the fire drill, but instead of defending himself and placing the blame on his chatty students in line, Mr. Wood kept his mouth closed and took full responsibility, knowing he was the teacher and they were his students.

"Go easy on yourself, Mr. Wood. You're doing a great job. Besides, she's like that for both of her sons."

14

FOOL'S GOLD

THE SMELL of used oil and brake fluid filled the dimly lit fifteen-car garage of the Junkyard at FATs University. Used tires were stacked neatly, and brooms stood at attention on the walls over sparkling linoleum floors. There was an old tin sign that read, *Everyone thinks they're a mechanic until their car doesn't start.* There wasn't a single tool out of place — each had a home. The upkeep of the garage had been strictly enforced at the Junkyard, and students were held accountable because safety always came first.

Similar to the chemistry labs in the science department and the rooms full of test dummies students use to learn how to administer CPR, the garage in the Junkyard was an oasis for would-be mechanics looking to learn everything about cars and what they have the potential to do.

The light from underneath the closed garage doors crept up to Mark's untied boots. He hadn't sat down since he left his dorm, and now he stood craning into the hood of his antique muscle car. In one hand he held his phone showing a how-to video of draining the radiator fluid, and in the other hand he held a flashlight to locate the petcock to drain its contents.

"Be sure the parking brake is up and your car jacks are securely underneath your automobile to prevent injury or death."

Where is this dang thing?

"Oh, Marky?!" a voice rang out from one of the doorways to the shop. "Who would've thought the first-place finisher would not only make it to class the morning after winning all of that money, but show up early, too?!"

Without lifting his head from the engine bay, Mark replied, "C'mon now, Caesar. Scholarship first."

"Too bad all those winnings can't help you flush that radiator fluid for today's exam!"

Mark cranked at the stubborn nut on the shut-off valve with his five-eighteenths socket wrench and laughed. "And how do you know exactly what's going to be on the exam, bro?"

"I've got my sources," Caesar said confidently, folding his arms.

"Oh yeah?" Mark said, nearly out of breath. "And who are these sources?"

"Whoa! Whoa!" Caesar spat as he began to pace around Mark's car. "I can't put them at risk like that."

Mark sucked his teeth and flicked overspill at his classmate as the old radiator fluid drained into a shop pan.

"At first, I was thinking the exam was going to be on changing the brakes," Caesar said, crouching down to eye his reflection in Mark's chrome rims, "but then he kept hinting towards the upkeep of the radiator and its effect on the temperature of the car."

"You sound afraid." Mark laughed. "I thought you said you were the top mechanic in this program?"

"I don't know what you're talking about."

"Oh yeah? That's not how you were sounding as you were making friends at the track last night."

"Well, I wasn't lying," Caesar said, peeking into Mark's front seat through the rolled-down tinted windows. "But in the case that the exam is on the radiator flush, you got me, buddy?"

Releasing the pressure from the valve before closing it and pouring in new fluid, Mark looked at Caesar and then looked down at his hands near his pockets. "This isn't a pen-and-paper exam, you know."

Caesar shifted his eyes as he moved his hands from his pockets and backed away from Mark's car. "Just hear me out. I might be willing to pay."

Mark contemplated as he reached for a shop towel.

"See, we got the same color car. And the professor is old, so when he looks away we switch places. After you finish your car, of course—"

Knock knock.

"Hey, boys," Regina greeted, carrying a basket and two custom sandwiches from the nearby supermarket. "I thought you'd be in here, Marcus."

"Mmhmm. Smells like hot-pressed subs—"

"Turkey and pepperoni with extra provolone."

"You know me so well." Mark smiled, entranced by his girlfriend.

"What I don't know is why you didn't answer my calls last night," Regina pressed, cutting straight to it. "Were you out racing last night, Marcus? You know how reckless that is."

"And profitable," Caesar cut in quietly.

"Shouldn't you be studying for the same exam Mark has in about forty-five minutes?" Regina replied, turning her attention and rolling her eyes.

"You know, I said the same thing!"

Caesar's face wrinkled like laundry as he motioned toward the door, forced to think of another way to pass the upcoming midterm. "I get it. I get it. You guys want some alone time. I'm leaving. Think about it, though, Mark."

15

THE RUMBLE NEAR THE RED JUNGLE GYM

THE SUN WAS relentless as the fourth-grade class of Three Pyramids Elementary School spilled onto the blacktop for recess. Basketballs and jump ropes lay like land mines waiting to scorch the hands of unsuspecting kids.

The wall was hot and unsupervised as Monte and Bao took their places, hoping their time would go by fast.

"Is there something you want to tell me, bro?"

"No!" Monte replied swiftly.

"You know you can tell me anything right, Monte?"

Monte dropped his eyes as Bao tried to meet his gaze. He thought of the truth in telling him that he had probably dropped it earlier that morning and Gus had most likely stolen it. He also thought of what comes after admitting the truth and the potential that Bao would rub it in that he loses everything.

Monte believed otherwise, though, and was convinced that finding Gus would get back the Tiger's Eye without ever having to tell Bao about losing it.

"I can't believe this," Bao complained as he motioned at their circumstances, granting Monte a merciful change of subject. "You know I've never even been on the wall before?"

"I wouldn't say this is my first time here," Monte replied after a pause. "But it's only for a few minutes. We'll be all right."

"Hey! Where's the soccer ball?" shouted one of the students from a neighboring fourth-grade class.

"Yeah! And the football, too?" another shouted from afar at Mr. Bolt as he towered over the crowd of kids growing anxious by the second.

"Okay, okay," the P.E. teacher said in a calming voice. "There'll be no use of the field for today's recess."

"But whhyyy?" they all groaned.

Putting his hands on his hips, Mr. Bolt sighed deeply and said, "Can't you guys see that they're prepping the field for tonight's fall festival?"

"Yeah, but they aren't using the whole field, coach," pressed Darren.

Mr. Bolt cut his eyes at one of the twins while furrowing his brows.

"Look at them." Monte nodded. "They don't know what to do without the soccer ball."

Bao laughed, looking at his watch.

"Has it been five minutes yet?" Monte quizzed.

"Who said you two aren't on this wall for the entire recess?" Mr. Wood said, appearing from the open hallway door.

"Whoa, were you hiding, Mr. Wood?" Bao said, backing away from the side door.

"Maybe I was, maybe I wasn't," Mr. Wood said, squinting his eyes. "I see I have to watch you two."

"We're just growing boys, Mr. Wood," Monte said, smiling in the sunshine. "Sometimes we make mistakes."

"Make less mistakes then, Montellous."

Monte lowered his head to avoid getting into deeper trouble.

"I expect better from you two," Mr. Wood said, folding his arms. "I've told you before, and I'll continue to say it. You two are my leaders of the class, so if they see you acting up," Mr. Wood paused to cut his eyes at Monte, "if they see you acting up, they'll think it's ok to, too."

Monte's eyes scanned the asphalt.

"Next time, we won't be 'talking this out' on the wall," Mr. Wood said, using his fingers as air quotations. "We'll be talking this out in the principal's office."

"Yes, sir," the boys replied as one.

Mr. Wood stayed silent as he drew out the suspense of Bao and Monte waiting to be released. They could tell by the break in his "do better" speech that he was about to let them go, but Monte could no longer fight the urge to speak out.

"C'mon, Mr. Wood. Don't hold us back from a good time out there," he pleaded.

"Oh, is that what I'm doing?" Mr. Wood replied, mock-confused. "Don't you think you earned this opportunity to stand here and think of your recent poor decisions?"

"Huh?" Bao questioned. "You make this sound like a reward."

"Well, tell them what they've won, Johnny!" Mr. Wood shouted, laughing at his own joke.

Monte and Bao looked at one another without a smile, and after an intentional awkward moment, Mr. Wood dismissed them.

A few minutes later, though Monte found humor in adding on to the laundry list of complaints still being thrown at Mr. Bolt; he cut through the jeers with, "But we can still shoot hoops, right? Because I'll school *all* y'all out here!"

"Ha! Yeah, right," retorted Brandon while rolling his eyes and nudging Richard. "Are you hearing this guy?"

As though he had wings, Monte leapt onto one of the black picnic tables that no one ever ate lunch on, stretched both arms out wide and said, "Get your team then, Brandon! I've been waiting on this all year."

MICHAEL A. WOODWARD, JR.

"Ohhh!" all of the fourth-grade boys and girls shouted as Brandon climbed atop the same picnic bench and now stood nose to nose with Monte.

"I'm on Monte's team!" one student called.

"I'm on Brandon's!" another countered.

"You boys get down from there!" Mr. Bolt shouted.

But the chanting of "Monte! Monte! Monte!" and "Brandon! Brandon!" drowned out the empty threats of the P.E. teacher.

Similar to the first day of that year, the fourth-graders began to divide themselves up, except this division was completely voluntary, and there were no administrators to tell them exactly where they belonged. As sides were taken, Mr. Wood took notice of the commotion just outside the jungle gym. Crossing his arms, he wasn't the least bit surprised to see Monte at the center of it.

Looking just over Brandon's shoulder, Monte noticed Mr. Wood speed-walking toward them.

"Is this how you all plan on spending these twenty minutes of recess — arguing?" Mr. Wood scolded, looking at his gold watch.

"We were just trying to play soccer, Mr. Wood." A kid whimpered from the crowd.

"You guys don't see those dump trucks pulling up to begin setting up for tonight's festival?" Mr. Wood questioned while shifting his eye contact among all of the boys surrounding him.

They all sucked their teeth and rolled their eyes.

"Yeah, so instead Brandon's gotta settle for a beat-down in a different sport."

"And his friends, too!" shouted one of the twins standing at Monte's feet.

Mr. Wood and Mr. Bolt made eye contact with one another as the tension built between Monte and Brandon's teams.

"All right, all right, are you boys going to dance battle up there, or are you going to play some ball?" Mr. Wood demanded as he made a gesture to Monte and Brandon to get down from the steel picnic table.

Brandon leaned in closer to Monte.

"You sure this is what you want, Montellous? You sure you want to see how we Northside kids get down at this school? Because I'm about to send you and your B Pod homies back to where you all belong."

Monte raised his eyebrows and inhaled deeply. Brandon's words were beginning to pierce the shield Monte used as a barrier for people's ignorance. His mother had taught him to do so after she had been a victim of hate and ill will. They had been in the grocery store together when the produce manager told her to go pick her own fresh vegetables beside the garbage can where she was born.

Monte had been only about six at the time, but he had seen the pain in his mother's eyes from the encounter. *Sometimes it's gonna be hard to be great, King. But you mustn't ever forget to be that — a king.* The next thing Monte knew, the produce manager had had a face full of unwashed cilantro and Italian parsley.

"You ready, Southside boy?"

Monte's blood was now boiling as he clenched his fists by his sides. The corner of his left eye was beginning to twitch, undercutting the calmness he intentionally portrayed to others while his lip began to curl, as well.

He climbed down without taking his eyes off Brandon.

Brandon did the same while flaring his nostrils.

Bao took notice of Monte's change of mood judging by his cold stare directed towards his classroom nemesis. He stepped into the crowd and met Monte on the concrete to show support for his best friend just as he had done a few weeks back to the Gimme Some Gang.

"Well, what're we waiting on?" shouted David while scrunching his face at Brandon and his crew just over Monte's shoulder.

"I was wondering the same thing," joked Mr. Bolt as he heaved worn basketballs over the fence onto the basketball courts.

At once, the other fourth-grade boys all darted toward the courts, but Monte and Brandon's teams hadn't moved a muscle, still staring at one another.

"You know I'm going to embarrass you in front of everyone out here, Montellous?"

"The only thing that's embarrassing is how you think everyone is beneath you."

"That's because they are," sneered Brandon. "Especially you. You're not even supposed to be in the honors program."

MICHAEL A. WOODWARD, JR.

"I deserve to be here. I earned my seat. You, on the other hand... we all know what got you into the honors program — and it sure isn't your reading."

"Ohhhh!" jeered the twins.

"Shoot, I deserve to be in the honors program, too!" shouted Darren.

Monte shot a puzzled yet supportive look. As though it was cool to be in the honors program. He was confused and happy to hear one of his closest friends from the Southside neighborhood admit to his academic aspirations.

"Oh, brother," Brandon scoffed, leaping from the tabletop. "We'll be on the courts, twerps. You guys draw straws or something to get down to three and we'll play to three."

Accepting the challenge, Monte nodded and turned to his crew. "Let's show them how we get down in the Southside."

16

NO FOUL

THE BLEACHERS WERE at capacity as children stood shoulder to shoulder screaming. Colorful sneakers crowded the faded yellow lines that outlined the perimeter of Three Pyramids' basketball courts. Some stood on top of, nearly covering, the out-of-bounds line, and others stood at the baseline, just under the goal. Somehow, Sneaky Steve had pre-popped plastic-bagged popcorn for sale that came in handy for the event. The roar of the student body echoed as a few of the carnival workers, sandwiches and thermoses in hand, tapped one another at the commotion from across the blacktop.

"Let's go!" one kid shouted.

"C'mon now, we don't have all recess!" another demanded.

"You guard Richard, Bao, and you take Jeff, Darren," coached Monte as the three boys huddled together at the free-throw line making a game plan. "Remember, keep Jeff out of the corner because all he'll do is stand there and wait for the three."

"I know, I know," Darren said proudly. "I got him. Have you ever played against these guys, Monte?"

"I've seen Brandon play at the park before against some older kids, but I've never seen that other kid from the Northside, Richard, play," Monte said, looking over his shoulder to watch him as he swished another mid-range shot from the top of the key. "I bet he's probably a scrub in the game, though."

"He hasn't missed!" David said with fear in his voice.

"It doesn't matter," Bao replied, taking off his glasses and turning to Monte. "You just keep your cool and watch those bricks you throw up from time to time."

Monte cut his eyes at his friend. His heart rate had been on the rise since he stood on the picnic tables in front of his peers. Seemingly, there were even more kids surrounding them now on the basketball courts. The crowd had swelled to the entire fourth grade.

"Y'all got these guys!" David said, putting his hand in the center of the huddle and making his case once more. "Now don't forget you can sub me in if you need me, though. I'll be right over there on the sideline."

"Scram, little bro," Darren scoffed, laughing and bumping shoulders with his younger twin by seven minutes. "We're trying to win, man."

"How about you just hype the crowd, bro," Monte consoled through his smile. "And make sure Nathalie sees, too."

Bao rolled his eyes.

"Are we doing this or not," Brandon said, shouting over the crowd and retrieving a royal-blue headband from his pocket. "Whatever plan you think you all have, it's not going to work."

"Let's do this, bros."

"Check," Monte said, bounce-passing the ball to Brandon.

"I've got your check," Brandon spat, striking the cement with the basketball. "I've been waiting for this for a long time, Southside boy."

"I never met someone in such a rush to lose at something."

Curling his lip, Brandon crossed the ball between his legs and made a move to his left in search of Jeff at the wing.

"I see you, bro!" David yelled from the sidelines.

"Nope," Monte said with his hands spread and knees bent in a defensive stance. "We know that game."

Nearly smothered, Brandon turned to conceal the ball while catching the eye of Richard, who caught the signal.

"Oh yeah?" Brandon said, smirking and looking to the crowd while throwing a no-look pass to Richard, who was cutting to the basket.

The crowd went insane as popcorn flew in the air.

"C'mon, Bao," Monte said, kicking the kernels that landed near his feet.

"That's one, Montellous," Brandon said with his finger in the air. "Two more and that's game."

"Well, I knew something had to make up for your reading," Monte replied.

Embarrassed, Brandon's eyes widened, then his eyebrows lowered. He checked the ball to Monte with nearly all of his might, but Monte caught it just in time. He gripped the black grooves on the ball and looked back at Brandon, awaiting an apology that never came.

"You gonna check it back or not?"

"I wanted to give you a moment to think about what you're getting yourself into, sir," Monte replied, rolling the ball at Brandon's feet.

In one motion, Brandon nodded his head as he bent down and passed the ball to Jeff making his way to his sweet spot. Motioning to defend, Monte was met by a brick wall of a pick Richard had set.

"Ohh!" the crowd called, wincing at Monte's agony.

"That had to hurt!" someone yelled.

"You shouldn't even be here on the court with me," Brandon said, his voice lowered to a whisper. "Just like how you shouldn't be in the honors program."

Swish!

The sound of the bottom of the net cut through the hum of the crowd like a knife through warm bread. Jeff and Richard bickered back and forth as Darren high-fived his twin brother. Bao, still standing behind the faded three-point line with his pinky up and wrist flicked, turned to Monte and said, "Get your head in the game, man."

"That's two, good sir," Monte said, turning back to his foe. "One more and *that's* game."

Brandon was fuming as his nostrils began to balloon — opening and closing, opening and closing. He checked the ball even harder than before to Monte, who almost didn't catch it this time.

"Bro!?" Monte said, turning to Bao and nearly squeezing the air out of the basketball. "He's asking for it!"

"Be in control, man," Bao said, calmly raising and lowering his palms at his waist. "Just be cool."

Monte took in a breath of the crisp fall air and made a crossover move, tilting his head in the opposite direction to fool Brandon. It had nearly worked, but Brandon adjusted and jabbed his forearm into Monte's side, turning him slightly. Monte began to back Brandon down as he lowered his hips and bounced the ball more quickly.

"You got 'em, Monte!" Nathalie yelled.

"Yeah! Take him to the hole!" Lizbeth shouted.

Inching his way to the goal, Monte was in striking distance of making a move to the basket. With buckled knees, Brandon was trying his best to match Monte's force but simply couldn't.

"I'm not letting you take this shot, Montellous."

"You can't stop me," Monte said, shifting his weight and preparing for his attack. "This is the end of the line for you."

"That's what you think," Brandon said under his breath as he felt Monte prepare to launch his body into the air. Without even going for the ball, Brandon lowered his shoulder and drove his elbow directly into Monte as he began to take flight. "Not today!"

Splat!

An eerie silence swept over the court as the ball bounced out of bounds. Monte lay motionless as Brandon attempted to play off the foul by stumbling for possession. Bao and the twins ran over to Monte. His eyes were closed and his breathing had slowed. Monte lay at Bao's feet as he bent down, snapping his fingers near Monte's ear. Nothing. Then, in an instant, Monte's eyelids shot open in rage, revealing bloodshot eyes that appeared possessed.

The crowd *oooh*ed, instigating as Monte fought through the pain to rise to his feet and hobble to the top of the key.

"You ok, bro?" Bao said, leaning in to Monte's ear.

Monte nodded, staring directly at Brandon. "Foul," he said, reaching out to Brandon for the ball.

"Get out of here. You knocked the ball out of bounds after you tripped and fell. No foul."

"It's our ball, Brandon, stop trying to prolong this."

"You want the ball, Montellous?!"

Monte held out his hands.

"Well, here!" Brandon shouted as he threw the ball with all of his might. "Have it!"

This time was different. Monte caught the ball yet again but flicked it back at Brandon right through his hands.

Smack!

Like a river, the blood began to flow through Brandon's nose as he fell to his knees, cupping his hands to catch the droplets. He used his shirt to help but was overtaken and began to cry hysterically.

The eerie silence returned as Brandon climbed to his feet and ran away in shame with Jeff and Richard trailing after him.

Monte hung his head, knowing his fate, as the bell rang signaling the end of recess.

17

NO EXCUSES

THE LUNCHROOM WAS BUSTLING as usual during this time of day. The assembly line of white Styrofoam plates was in full force as trash cans wheeled through the rows of cafeteria tables. Milk splattered and syrup made napkins stick to the table as the fourth-graders peered through the cafeteria windows.

"Mhmmm, smells like cinnamon French toast sticks, bro."

"Yeah!" Darren replied, already over the game. "I'm starving, anyway—"

"Boys," Nathalie interrupted, inserting herself into the conversation. "Where's Monte?"

At the sharpness in Nathalie's question, the twins and Bao all looked at one another as they hesitated to tell her, knowing she was going to give Monte a piece of her mind.

"I'm waiting," she said, crossing her arms and shifting her weight onto her back foot.

The twins shrugged with their lips sealed.

Bao motioned his head without moving the rest of his body. His eyes shifted in the direction of the blacktop.

"Now, that wasn't so hard, was it?" Nathalie sarcastically remarked as she glared at the twins.

Choosing not to respond, Darren looked directly at Bao. "Why would you tell her where he is? You know she's going to give it to him!"

Bao didn't respond immediately; he didn't even look Darren's way. After a moment, however, he stopped staring through the tinted windows and spoke. "Monte knows what he did, Darren." He turned and completely faced his friend now. "He felt embarrassed and made the wrong decision—"

"We were all embarrassed!"

"I didn't even play, and I'm embarrassed," quipped David.

"None of that even matters," Bao said with a shrug. "Just because you don't get the foul doesn't give you the right to bust a kid's nose open. I mean, c'mon, there was blood everywhere — just look at your shoes!"

Craning their necks, the twins looked down at the edge of Darren's left shoe.

Bao breathed out deeply, lowered his tense shoulders and walked away, saying, "I'm not even really hungry anymore."

There were no further excuses to be made.

18

I THOUGHT I KNEW YOU

"MONTE!

Monteeee?

Montellous!?!"

Where is this boy? Nathalie thought.

Monte heard her between the clanging sounds of tin roofs for the carnival booths and the sound of chairs and picnic tables being loaded out of flatbeds. Monte heard her shrill voice quite clearly. He just chose not to respond.

Nathalie was persistent, though, which was what Monte liked most about her. He'd always taken notice of how she'd try at something over and over again until she mastered it.

As he swung slowly with both of his hands raised and gripped tightly around the rusted chain links of the swing set, his head hung low as he recalled the memories of Nathalie and her attempts at mastering the art of reading during their small groups in first grade. Whether because of elementary love or showmanship, Nathalie inspired Monte to be a better scholar than he ever saw himself as. He was a scholar to his mother and father, or else he'd get in big trouble, but to Nathalie he was a scholar for a totally different reason. But right now the love that Nathalie had for Monte was shared in a very different way than Monte was used to from her.

"So you didn't hear me, Montellous?"

Monte shrugged and kept his eyes fixed on the tiny black dots sprinkled across the playground turf. Although he heard the soles of her feet shuffling nearer and saw her approaching from the corner of his eye, he kept his hood over his head in shame.

"Who are you becoming?"

Still silent, Monte removed his hands from the rusted chains and tucked them into his armpits as though he were a little child.

"Look at you! You're bleeding, boy."

"So what?" Monte said, now standing and trying his best to conceal his embarrassment. "He had it coming!"

"Why?!" Nathalie demanded, already knowing the answer. "Because you were losing a silly game of basketball in front of the entire fourth grade?"

"He pushed me, though!" He pushed back his sleeves, exposing the blood that dripped down to his wrists from the scrapes on his elbows. "I can't go for that."

"Why, because you think it makes you look soft, huh?"

Monte rolled his eyes and sucked his teeth.

"Oh, I get it. You gotta be the man in the honors program like you're the man in the Southside neighborhood, right?"

"Whatever, Nathalie. Brandon got what he deserved."

"But who makes you the judge and jury, though?" Nathalie questioned unapologetically.

"You think you know me so well."

"I know you're a much bigger person than who you were out there on the basketball court."

Monte wrinkled his forehead and looked over to the scene of the crime where Nathalie was pointing. A sense of guilt began to creep down his spine as he noticed the trail of Brandon's blood from the three-point line to near where they were standing. Quickly tucking away the disappointment in himself, Monte slipped his hands inside his jean jacket pockets.

"You didn't have to embarrass Brandon like that, Monte. You're better than that, and you know it."

"He was just mad disrespectful, ok!?"

"So?!" Nathalie spat out with her arms now folded. "Stop saying that. That doesn't justify ever hitting anyone."

"Whatever, yo."

Nathalie stepped closer as she held stern eye contact, hiding the softer side of her true feelings.

"Don't 'whatever' me!" Nathalie barked. "All of the boys in the B Pod follow your lead, and it's your choice whether you inspire them to be as incredible as I see you as or not."

Avoiding her gleaming eyes, he thought of down-playing what she was saying. Although Monte was equipped with all of the confidence in the world, he was still human. He was still fully aware of the differences he faced for being a young Black boy in certain spaces. There were times where Monte tried to fool himself into believing he was just another kid at Three Pyramids Elementary, but deep down he and Nathalie both knew that there was something special in Monte that everyone saw.

"Are we done here, Nat?"

Clenching her fists and getting nearly as mad as Monte was, Nathalie took a deep breath. She hated when people shortened her name, and Monte knew that.

She found a sense of relief from the moment as the carnival music began to play in the background. It was eerie in a way, as it resembled the funhouses she had feared most as a child, but calming as the more she exchanged with Monte the angrier she was getting.

"I thought you truly were a king, Montellous, but maybe you are just a prince."

That cut Monte like a knife through fresh fruit. He stood speechless as his pride withered.

"I hope one day you truly realize the impact you have on people, Monte. Especially the kids that call themselves your friends. You walk around like you're the man, but your actions speak otherwise."

"You don't know what you're talking about."

"Oh, I do!" spat Nathalie. "I saw the way you treated that kindergartener during the fire drill."

Monte's eyes shifted.

"I thought I saw something special in you, but obviously not. I can't even look at you right now. Matter of fact, I think we're through here. Goodbye, Montellous."

No friend had ever spoken to him the way Nathalie just had. It took all of his might to keep his cool, but he couldn't hide how deep his curly-haired crush's words had cut him. He wanted to defend himself and argue back with her, but he couldn't. He knew she was right. He knew he could've made better decisions as he was certain the Tiger's Eye would have guided him to.

19

DO BETTER

THE ORANGE and yellow leaves whipped around Monte's knees as he kicked one of the faded basketballs that lay on the blacktop.

As he licked the dried blood from his wrists, Monte took a moment to collect himself before heading towards the cafeteria to face his peers and, eventually, Mr. Wood and Dr. Styles.

He took a deep breath and put his hands behind his head to allow in as much of the cool fall air as his lungs would allow.

The swings drifted slowly, as did the tetherballs that hung from the unraveling ropes that hadn't been replaced in years.

In the distance, several grounds crews balanced bales of hay and pieced together the merry-go-round, yet Monte felt alone.

Up above, a lone cloud cast a shadow of embarrassment over Monte; deep down, he knew he was wrong and regretted nearly every decision that he had made that day — including losing the Tiger's Eye.

As Monte approached the glass doors to the cafeteria, he caught a glimpse of his reflection. His hand grabbed at the handle, but he couldn't find the strength to look away from himself.

Who am I becoming? he thought.

Bao saw Monte staring at himself from the other side of the glass and immediately excused himself from the lunch table.

Already knowing the answer, he asked his best friend anyway to show that he was there for him, "You ok, bro?"

"I'm alright."

Bao stayed quiet allowing room for Monte to say more. "I saw you out here with Nathalie, so I gave you your space to be with your girl."

"That's not my girl anymore."

"I see." Bao raised one of his eyebrows. "So... what was that on the court, bro? I knew you were getting mad, but I didn't think you were going to let Brandon have it like that."

Monte broke eye contact as he motioned past Bao toward the end of the lunch line while shrugging his shoulders.

Answering his own question, Bao replied, "Well, to be honest, I've been waiting for someone to do that for years."

The two boys laughed carelessly, as though they weren't aware of the trouble Monte would soon face.

"We've got a seat saved for you, bro." He pointed to the lunch table just over his shoulder. "Join us when you're ready."

"Thanks, Bao. You're a great friend, you know that, right?"

"Duh, that's what best friends are for."

Half-smiling, Monte said softly, "I know, bro. I know."

Monte stood alone at the end of the lunch line. Still throbbing, his elbow ached and bled even heavier with each bend that stretched his skin beneath his jacket. He soon realized that the more he grabbed at it, the more it began to bleed through his sleeves.

Monte seemed more put off the longer he stood with his back to the glass as he faced the rows of his onlooking peers.

He stood, embarrassed, and he felt them all talking about him — and not in the ways that he was used to. He reflected heavily on Nathalie's words as they repeated themselves over and over like a hot summer song on the radio.

I thought you truly were a king.

I thought I saw something special in you.

I thought I knew you.

I wonder who else I let down, Monte thought, suppressing his emotions.

As hard as it was to believe, Monte rarely found himself in trouble. He was as stubborn as a bull and incredibly rebellious at times, but somehow he usually flew under the radar when it came to getting into trouble.

Unfortunately, Monte's greatest weakness was his inability to overlook disrespectful people. He always treated people the way he wanted to be treated and stood up to those who failed to return the favor.

His ambition and charisma usually saved him from severe consequences, but this time was different. Yet as big and bad as he presented himself to be, Monte typically followed the rules.

The faces on the other kids in the lunchroom were telling, though. Monte thought that their shame in him radiated from above their trays along with their whispers of the 'rumble near the red jungle,' as he had heard a kid from another class say between his and Bao's exchange.

He knew for a fact that they were talking about him, but he couldn't quite make out if they were painting him as the good guy... or the bad guy within the gossip.

Monte's eyes continued to scan the room as he inched closer into the doorway where lunch was being served. He hadn't seen Brandon since he fled the courts crying, his face in his palms.

"I'll take the French toast sticks, please," Monte said while tapping on the sneeze-guard glass.

"Hands off the glass!" Mr. Jerry said while flinging shredded hash browns off the tongs he sometimes used as a pointer to emphasize his advice to students. "What's eating you, Monte? You look like a kid who just lost his house key and has to go home and face the music."

A smile slid its way to the corner of Monte's mouth. He knew that particular feeling all too well.

"There we go, young man!" Mr. Jerry clicked his tongs like applause and flashed an authentic game show host smile from behind the serving counter. "Life's too short to be mad at the world, son. Never let something or someone else control your emotions and make you feel how they want you to feel. Your mind must be strong!"

Monte held eye contact as Mr. Jerry's words struck a chord within him. He thought of the fear the dogs had made him feel early that morning. He thought of the rage he had allowed Brandon to bring about. But most of all, Monte thought of the mental strength Mrs. Heart-Moore had spoken about in class, when she'd expressed her confidence in him.

"Thanks, Mr. Jerry," Monte said as he reached for his plate of food, half-understanding and half-hungry. "I think I know what you mean."

Yet Mr. Jerry didn't let go of the plate. He held eye contact with Monte, who appeared inspired and ashamed all at once. As Mr. Jerry cleared his throat, making room for his deep baritone voice, he stopped smiling at Monte and held down the drawstrings from his chef's coat. He leaned in just over the steam that rose from the boiling water that warmed the food and said in a whisper, "Be the leader we all see you as, young man. Some of us who come from where we come from don't get the opportunity you have in that honors program."

"Yes, sir," Monte mouthed quietly as he broke eye contact. "I'll do my best."

"Sometimes, son... your best isn't good enough in life. Not if your best is what they're saying you did out there on the basketball courts."

Monte bit his lip and nodded as Mr. Jerry finally let go of the plate. He reached for the change in his pocket to pay for his food and turned back to see Mr. Jerry was still staring at him. "I'll do better, sir. I promise."

20

COLD FRENCH TOAST STICKS

BEFORE MONTE COULD MAKE it to the lunch table, there stood Dr. Styles at the doorway, scanning the lunchroom like a warden in jail. She pulled at the cuffs of her sleeves as her eyes danced from one table to the next in search of her inmate. There was a stiffness in her neck as her eyes found Monte's before he found his friends.

"Right this way, young man," Dr. Styles commanded. "Don't even put your lunch tray down."

Shuffling his feet, Monte bowed his head as the lunchroom fell silent. Standing but a few tables away, Monte felt as though it was the longest walk of his life toward the exit. He felt the eyes of the entire fourth-grade class as they all avoided eye contact when his would meet theirs. Everyone shared their disappointment in Monte, and he felt every bit of it. He wondered if this would be the last time he'd ever eat lunch with his friends or even attend Three Pyramids. Monte thought he was, for sure, going to get kicked out of the honors program.

"Stay strong, Monte!" one of the twins yelled out.

"Yeah! Stay strong, bro!" the other followed, catching the attention of their teacher, Miss Bleacher.

"Zip it! Or you two are next!"

Fleeing to the restroom in an attempt to avoid the scene, Nathalie excused herself from the table as she heard a knock.

"Gus?" Nathalie said, confused, while opening the door to the playground. "I don't remember seeing you out there at recess."

Slipping by nonchalantly, Gus tiptoed his way into the cafeteria while Monte was still the center of attention. *This is my chance,* Gus thought, heading for the remaining food of the lunch period.

"Wait, I don't even remember seeing you at the fire drill."

"Shouldn't you be worried about your king over there?" Gus said, raising his chin toward Monte making his walk of shame. "Looks like he's in the hot seat if you ask me."

Nathalie cut her eyes away behind her bouncy natural brown curls as Gus turned to the empty lunch line before she could respond.

"Dr. Styles, wait!" Monte said, seeing Gus maneuver his large frame through the near-closed door to the serving area. "Gus! He stole something from me earlier! Let me go and get it, please!"

"The only thing that's being stolen at the moment is my time, young man," Dr. Styles said, folding her arms. "You're already in hot water and you think I'm about to wait for you? Get your behind in that main office. *Now!*"

21

THE CALM BEFORE THE STORM

MONTE'S FEET swung from the cherry oak seat across from Mrs. Sheffield's desk in the main office. He hadn't touched the food that sat in front of him. His hash browns were now cold, and his cinnamon French toast sticks had begun to harden.

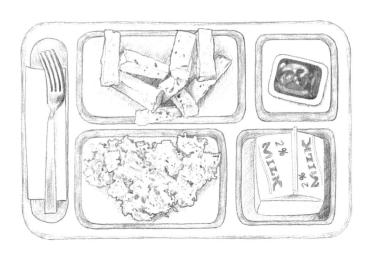

He could see a few drops of blood leading into Dr. Styles's office and knew by the bloody tissues in the trash can that the time had come to own up to his actions and be the king his family and close friends saw him as — or at least they *had*.

Monte felt the cold air from underneath Dr. Styles's office door nipping at his ankles below the seams of his jeans and reached to pull up his socks. He wondered if she intentionally kept her office like the Arctic for kids who got in trouble like him.

Clearly, this was new to Monte. He had never been pulled into the principal's office before. Truthfully, he had never gotten into this level of trouble at school. Sure, he'd fought before, but never at school, which made him immediately anxious of the possibility of expulsion — or worse, his father finding out.

Monte kept his hands insulated within his jacket. The hood he had put back up made him feel not only warm but hidden at times when he simply wanted to escape reality. Unfortunately, this wasn't one of those times where Monte had the luxury of deciding whether or not he wanted to be social — he was in the hot seat.

"Good afternoon, Mr. Wood," Mrs. Sheffield said softly over her double computer monitor as she typed away at the out-of-school suspension memo she had been ordered to create.

"Afternoon, ma'am," he responded as he marched directly over to his favorite student.

Yet in that moment Monte was far from being championed as such. Mr. Wood towered over Monte and tapped his cheaply made ballpoint pen on the dry wall as an outlet to keep his anger at bay. His eyebrows were scrunched together, and the repeated pitter patter of his left heel stated the rush of confusion and disappointment he was currently experiencing.

"Really?!" Mr. Wood said, refusing to conceal how he truly felt towards his scholar. "Really, really?"

Monte refused to raise his head and buried it as deeply as he could within what he wished were a cloak but was simply his jacket.

"You think you're supposed to be here, huh? Like we're supposed to put up with this and that the entire world revolves around you, huh?"

Monte shrugged, studying the back of the blue two-percent milk carton that lay sideways in front of him.

Mr. Wood lowered himself until he was at eye level with Monte. He invaded his entire personal space and made Monte feel incredibly uncomfortable. "You want to go to alternative school, huh? You really want to let your mother and those around you down. You want to go to cause mayhem and mischief and bully others, don't you? You want to end up in jail or, even worse, in a coffin?"

Monte didn't know how to respond to the flurry of questions that were thrown at him like punches in the twelfth round of a heavyweight bout.

A tear began to form in the well of one of his eyes. The weight of disappointment that was coming from everyone around him was beginning to overwhelm Monte.

Yet Mr. Wood was relentless at tearing down the pride of his star pupil. His eyebrows had gone from being scrunched together to making a fierce downward arrow that led directly to his flaring nostrils, which opened wider at each breath.

"Stop that! You can't be big and bad in front of your peers and cry because you're in the principal's office away from them. You made every single choice leading up to this very moment, and I couldn't be more saddened about them."

Monte's lip quivered as his nose begun to run while he dried his eyes.

"It's time to grow up and be held accountable for your actions," Mr. Wood said as he stood back up and slowly shook his head in the now-familiar way he had barely an hour ago. "I can't even believe you right now, Montellous."

"I'm sorry, Mr—"

"I don't want to hear it!" Mr. Wood shouted as he snatched down Monte's hood that draped over his ears. "A man only apologizes when he truly means it, and right now I just don't think you do, sir."

Monte sank in his seat as he caught Mrs. Sheffield's eyes nearly popping out of their sockets. A subtle "hmph" could be heard as she continued to fiercely peck away at her keyboard, but she never looked up from her monitor.

Suddenly, Dr. Styles's door creaked open, letting out more cold air that swept through the narrow hallway that led to it. "Mr. Wood, is that you?" a voice called out from inside. "If so, come in and bring in Mr. Driarson."

"Yes, ma'am," Mr. Wood replied, yet to break his cold stare at Monte. "Gather yourself and let's go."

Monte took in a deep breath before standing up, not exactly knowing his fate. He left behind his breakfast-food lunch, dried his eyes and stood tall.

The two products of the Southside neighborhood walked one after the other down the narrow hallway that led to the principal's office. Mr. Wood's eyes were fixed directly in front of him as Monte trailed slowly behind him, counting the tiles on the floor.

The door was slightly ajar as the two of them approached and before raising his hand to push the door fully open, Mr. Wood took one final look at his favorite honors student and said, "Be mature in there, Montellous, and keep your head held high."

Slowly, Monte nodded, but only once as Mr. Wood didn't wait for him to respond.

22

THE PRINCIPAL'S OFFICE

THE SHELVES that decorated the principal's office were crowded with elephants with their trunks up. There were small elephants, big elephants, crimson-colored elephants, young elephants, old elephants, books of elephants, and even miniature glass elephants that dotted all available space.

Endless framed college degrees and certificates hung proudly from above her huge red leather chair, in which she rocked back and forth. Mr. Wood positioned himself, calmly, against Dr. Styles's bookshelf near the window portraying parent pick up.

Brandon was sitting in one of the two chairs in front of the desk. He was still wiping at his nose and eyes. He didn't look over at Monte, but he didn't need to for Monte to see the damage he had caused both physically and emotionally.

Silence filled the air as elephants, who were somehow positioned in toy double-decker airplanes hanging from the ceiling, circled above them.

Folding his arms to fight the cold, Monte focused on a spot just above Dr. Styles's left shoulder in an attempt to find his happy place to avoid getting deeper into trouble. He had learned this trick from Mark, who was notorious for being in the hot seat with their parents.

In an attempt to mentor Monte, as he had from time to time, he had once said, "Little brother, the only way to avoid getting into more trouble when you're already in trouble is to keep a straight face, simply respond 'yes, ma'am, no, ma'am,' and find your happy place on the wall. Never, ever talk back."

Mr. Wood put his hands in his blue slacks and stared directly at Monte, who pretended not to see.

Dr. Styles leaned in, connecting the tips of her fingers and placing her chin in the space between her thumbs and pointer fingers, "Well, gentlemen, I must say, bravo. You nearly started a riot on the basketball courts, put your hands on one another —

and on top of that, I nearly decided to place the entire grade level on silent lunch for the rest of the week. What could you possibly have to say for yourselves?"

Immediately, Brandon protested by pleading his case, pointing at Monte. "It's his fault! He's the reason I'm still bleeding and the reason I'm in here. He's been trouble since the first day of classes, and I don't think he should even be in the honors program. He doesn't even want to be in it and slows us down anyway—"

"That's more than enough, Mr. Wells," Dr. Styles said, cutting in and stopping Brandon as he stood in protest against his peer.

Dr. Styles looked over at Mr. Wood as he breathed deeply, in through his nose and out through his mouth.

"So you're saying you had played no part in any of the events that took place today, Mr. Wells?"

"Not the slightest!"

"Is that so?" Dr. Styles remarked, half-spinning her chair to turn to a surprised Mr. Wood. "Not the slightest, he says."

"Well, I guess that settles it," Dr. Styles said. "Go see the nurse to clean yourself up and return to lunch."

Mr. Wood folded his arms as he looked out of the window. A familiar car was parking in the parent pick-up area.

"That's it?" Monte protested. "He says he's a victim and just like that you take the cuffs off and he can go?"

Dr. Styles sat back in her chair and rocked back and forth, unbothered.

"Don't worry yourself over the consequences of Brandon's actions, Monte; you've got much bigger problems."

Monte looked down to his lap to avoid rolling his eyes.

"Oh yes, you've led me to no other choice based upon *your* recent poor choices and lackluster efforts."

Knowing his father was working a double that day and the school would have been unable to get a hold of him, Monte relaxed a bit. He also knew his mother had an incredibly busy day today and in no way could make the time for a cameo at school before the festival, so he sat back in his chair and wisely remained silent.

"You've just been on a roll lately, huh, Monte?" Mr. Wood mused.

"I agree. Most recently, I've been seeing a different Montellous Driarson. You seem to be changing. Are the honors classes too much for you? Would you like to decommit from the program and go back to taking regular classes?" Dr. Styles said.

"I'm no quitter," Monte replied calmly. "I know I can do this."

"Are you certain?" Mr. Wood challenged.

I think I can, Monte thought. *I can do this, right? I mean, yeah, I could quit and be with my friends, but what about my best friend, Bao? I can't leave him by himself to deal with Brandon and Mr. Wood.* Monte looked up and nodded at Mr. Wood.

"I'm certain. I'd never quit on you," Monte replied. "Plus, my mom would never go for that."

Just then, Dr. Styles's office phone rang. "Ah, perfect timing, Mrs. Sheffield; send her on back."

Monte's heart skipped a beat as he sat up in his chair. "What's going on Dr. Styles? Who's coming back here?"

Mr. Wood cleared his throat and widened his eyes as there was a knock at the door.

"Come in!" Dr. Styles called invitingly. "Now that we're all here, what were you saying about your mother and your commitment to the honors program, Montellous?"

23

THE PARENT-TEACHER CONFERENCE

MRS. DRIARSON BURNED a hole into her son through the collar of Monte's torn denim jacket as he scratched at an itch on his neck that wasn't there. The folds in her forehead connected her furrowed eyebrows and disguised her gentle spirit in a way that could have easily been mistaken for rage.

Even on silent, her cell phone vibrated loudly in the designer purse Monte's father had recently spent his last dime on for her birthday. She'd told her boss she would only be gone for fifteen minutes, but that had been half an hour ago, and he had called twice already.

Refusing to put her purse on the floor, Mrs. Driarson placed it in her lap as she took up the empty chair next to her son, never once breaking her flinty stare. Her mouth was ajar, but she was silent; everyone in the room could tell she was still processing what exactly had happened.

"So, Montellous, what do you have to say for yourself?" Mr. Wood broke the ice, rubbing his stomach as he saw his eighteen-minute lunch period tick away.

Dr. Styles leaned forward over her clasped hands. Pinning her chin down, she looked at Monte directly in the eyes just above her red designer frames. Her eyelashes flicked rhythmically as she waited for Monte to speak.

Mrs. Driarson's neck craned as she gripped the brown leather straps of her purse tightly while awaiting her son's response.

"I mean—"

"Boy, don't lie!" his mother spat, causing Monte to flinch.

Mr. Wood chuckled silently to himself.

"I made a mistake."

"Oh, we know you made a mistake!" Mrs. Driarson interjected, muzzling her vibrating phone. "Got me lying to my boss to come here because you can't keep your hands to yourself."

"I didn't put my hands on anyone, Ma."

Inserting herself into the back and forth, Dr. Styles cut in, "I've noticed you've been making a number of mistakes lately, Monte."

Monte sank in his chair.

"As have I," said Mr. Wood, taking his turn at the interrogation. "What's really going on, King?"

Breaking her stare as the word "King" seeped into her ears, Mrs. Driarson breathed in and looked over at Mr. Wood as she thought back to his handwritten note to Monte.

She remembered his words of affirmation and the promise he'd made to Monte on the very first day of school to always be there for him. She had known from the beginning that this teacher was different and was exactly what her youngest son needed in his life. Mrs. Driarson eased up a smidge.

Oblivious to his mother's shift, Monte silently continued to deflect eye contact to keep his composure.

"Hello?! I know you hear that man talking to you, Montellous."

Dr. Styles raised her eyebrows in a bit of fear herself.

"I've just been going through some things, Ma."

"Some things like what?" She gripped the arms of her chair. "Please, do tell us."

"If there's something you want to let us know, Montellous, you know you can tell us anything," Dr. Styles said as she reached out for Monte's hands on her desk.

Slowly, Monte pulled them back and placed them in his pockets in search of his quartz crystal that wasn't there.

This isn't getting me anywhere, Monte thought. *I've gotta get out of this before it gets ugly.*

"Someone took something of mine, and I've just been in a funk ever since."

"Is that why you were on the floor this morning scanning the carpet for something you lost—"

"I didn't lose it, Mr. Wood — it was taken from me."

"Is this the reason why you seemed to have a difficult time with the substitute yesterday, Monte?"

"Excuse me?!" Mrs. Driarson exploded.

"Voices, please, you guys," Mr. Wood pleaded, flicking his eyes toward the office where Mrs. Sheffield was working.

Monte breathed in deeply and looked at three of the most important people in his life. He knew that he wasn't in trouble because they disliked him; he was in trouble because they cared about him.

He also knew that he was in the wrong for many of his actions. He had made some bad choices lately, and as he had heard his father tell Mark countless times, it was time for his chickens to come home to roost.

"I'm sorry for throwing the ball in Brandon's face. I could tell you it was because I think he thinks he's better than everyone from the Southside neighborhood, or that he refers to my friends in the B Pod as 'reduced lunch kids,' but I threw the ball mostly because we were losing."

Mr. Wood rubbed his thighs with unease.

The three adults, who all had grown up in the Southside and had paid their forty cents a day for lunch, too, looked at one another somberly.

"I also apologize for being mean to the kinder-gartener this morning. I was just trying to look cool in front of Bao and keep a stupid lie going."

Dr. Styles shook her head.

"And the substitute?!" Mrs. Driarson spat out, dissatisfied. "Were you trying to look cool then, too?"

Monte nodded slowly in defeat.

"And when were you even going to share that with me? You had the opportunity to this morning, Montellous."

Monte lowered his voice to a whisper. "I wanted to tell you tomorrow – after the hayride."

"Hayride?! Mrs. Driarson scoffed. "I don't think you'll be making it to the Fall Festival Hayride this year, young king."

"Now, now, Mrs. Driarson," Mr. Wood said, now standing erect and putting out a placating hand. "Monte has worked awfully hard this year in my class, and I'd hate to see a few missteps in his deci-sion-making exclude him from the event."

Monte's eyebrows raised as he felt new air come into his lungs. *Did I just hear that right? Did he just stick up for me? After all I've done?* Monte thought, peeking at the reaction of his mother.

Mrs. Driarson's phone vibrated again as she folded her arms.

"How about we make a deal?" Dr. Styles offered.

"I like deals!" Monte said, sitting up in his chair.

Mrs. Driarson looked at her son in a way only an agitated mother could and softly said to Dr. Styles, "Go on."

Reaching into her red steel file cabinet just beside her knee, Dr. Styles flipped through alphabetically sorted Manila folders of students:

Dragic
Drayton
Driarson

Pulling the file, Dr. Styles placed it on her desk and immediately looked over at Mrs. Driarson.

"I thought the only folders of students were at the front with Mrs. Sheffield," Monte asked in an attempt at making small talk.

"Mrs. Sheffield is the keeper of all records; these are nothing more than copies of the files of special students I like to keep my eye on," Dr. Styles said slyly, grinning at Monte as she refocused her attention.

Special students? Monte thought as his stomach twisted and began to knot.

Opening the folder to display the contents to everyone present, Dr. Styles began to read from the papers as she flipped through them.

"Kindergarten. All As in studies and conduct. First grade. All A-minuses in studies and all Bs in conduct."

She made a small "hmph," continuing to flip through.

"Second grade. All As and Bs in studies and Bs and Cs in conduct."

"Oh, I remember that year quite clearly," Mrs. Driarson said, cutting her eyes at her son, who sat wide-eyed like a deer in headlights.

"Reading award, Random Act of Kindness Award, voted most likely to lead by his peers in third grade—"

"My man!" Mr. Wood cut in with a smile.

Dr. Styles looked over her shoulder to calm her teacher's over-excitement.

"Third grade, As, Bs and a C in your studies." She repeated herself pointedly, "As, Bs, and a C, Monte."

"Oh, he knows how we feel about Cs in our household, isn't that right, Montellous?"

Biting his tongue to avoid from making excuses about the in and out subs of third grade and how that had impacted his reading and math skills, he looked at Mr. Wood.

Slowly shaking his head and mouthing a *shhh* sound with his lips, Mr. Wood cued Monte to stay quiet.

"Now, let's not forget about Ms. Pringle leaving Monte's class on the very first day of that year. For the entire—"

"We are aware of the revolving door of substitute teachers Monte and his class faced last year, sir," Dr. Styles said, wrapping up Mr. Wood's point for him.

Subtly winking at Monte, Mr. Wood retreated.

"Now, before Mrs. Driarson's phone vibrates again and the lunch bell rings, back to my proposition."

"Sit up," Mrs. Driarson said, patting her son's knee rhythmically.

"It's clear to us all that you are a not only a scholar but a leader, as well, Montellous. You are a shining star at this school, but you have to hold yourself more accountable for your thoughts and actions. You know I have every right to expel you, not only from the honors program but from Three Pyramids as a whole..."

Monte's heart began to race. *Get outta here.* His breath ran short. *She wouldn't.*

That feeling of love and care brought about from Dr. Styles just a moment ago had taken a sharp turn in the very same breath.

Her words rolled off coldly, as though a decision had already been made, and in that moment Monte thought that there was no small-talking his way out of this one.

Mr. Wood nodded in agreement as Dr. Styles pulled out a single sheet of paper from the bottom of the stack of accolades and report cards. She placed the Manila folder back behind Lamar Drayton's and slid the contract directly to Monte.

"Read this carefully and sign it," Dr. Styles offered. "If you decline then you will serve a five day out-of-school suspension and will be dismissed from the honors program effective immediately."

Monte picked up the contract and read it slowly to himself.

I, _____, understand that I am much better than the poor choices I have made lately. I know that there are consequences to all of my actions and will follow the ones set forth within this contract.

If I break any of the points listed below I will be removed from the TP Honors Program, effective immediately.

1: Attend 6 Counselling Sessions w/ Mrs. Heart-Moore.

2: Read to the kindergarteners once a week during recess.

3: Inspire the masses.

Monte looked over at his mother, and she responded with a look that said, *What is there to think about?*

24

POUR IT ON GENTLY

THE LIGHTS to the school nurse's bathroom came on automatically as Monte pushed the heavy door open.

"It's ok, Nurse Petty, I can clean myself up."

"Ok, baby; I'm right outside if you need me," Nurse Petty insisted as she set her bathroom keys down and reached for her vacation destination brochure.

"Sheesh," Monte whispered.

"What'd ya say?"

Monte's eyes widened. "Nothing, ma'am," he said, disappearing into the LED-lit bathroom.

For years he had been trying to pinpoint exactly who the school nurse reminded him of. She had led the annual hand-washing initiative for the school as personal hygiene week came and went.

During an open house, she once gave an impromptu live demonstration of the Heimlich maneuver to parents and families when someone's baby brother was choking on a green grape from a fruit tray.

For the most part, it was safe to say Nurse Petty was at the will of the community at Three Pyramids Elementary. She loved the children and adults dearly, but on the Monday or Tuesday following every holiday weekend, she would always leave her mini hand sanitizer hanging from her locked door and well wishes on her dry erase board.

In the past, Monte would see her standing outside of her office between classes but had really never needed a reason to visit her - Monte had never had even a scrape at school.

Snapping back to reality, Monte took off his jacket and reached for the jar of bandages and bottle of green isopropyl alcohol. He looked down at his scraped right elbow and already knew.

He took a knee on the glossy tile bathroom floor, rolled up his shirt sleeve to the top of his shoulder and stretched out his arm across the sink.

I can do this, Monte reassured himself as he braced for the sting.

Monte took a deep breath and popped open the same alcohol his grandmother used to pour on him when he would scrape his knee while learning to ride a bike.

The pain was unbearable, but the soothing sound of her angelic voice had always made it all feel better.

It's ok, baby, she would smile and say.

Be strong like the King we see you as.

Pain is temporary, but your battle scars will last forever.

Knowing there wasn't much to be proud of for these wounds, Monte took in another deep breath and counted to three.

"One... Two... *Ah!*"

"Montellous!" Nurse Petty said, storming into the bathroom. "Are you ok?!"

"The pain!" he wailed as the alcohol seeped into his open wound. "It stings so badly, Nurse Petty. Oh, it hurts!"

Nurse Petty reached for the cotton balls and commanded Monte to sit down on the little nursing cot in the room as she fanned her Cancun brochure at Monte's raw flesh.

"Breathe, baby, breathe," she said, blowing at his wounds. "Calm down."

The white paper crinkled as Monte winced atop the stiff blue bed. He wiped a tear as Mrs. Sheffield peeked her head into the nurse's bathroom. "Everything okay in here? I thought I heard a kindergartner in here screaming."

Nurse Petty allowed a small smile to slip through her curled lips.

Noticing, Monte managed to shoot a quick side eye in an attempt to mask his pain and embarrassment.

"Girl, you heard him, too? He was just yellin' and screamin'!" Nurse Petty cackled with laughter.

Monte's cheeks began to grow red as he opened the bandage packaging with his teeth, releasing a snarl.

"It's okay, Mr. Driarson," the school secretary dismissed Monte's false bravado. "As long as you promise to stay out of the principal's office, we won't tell anyone you were in here crying."

"C'mon, Mrs. Sheffield, you know I'm trying to make better choices."

"Uh-huh." Mrs. Sheffield drained the playfulness from her voice. "It sounds good, Monte, but that's not what Dr. Styles sees, what I see, and certainly not what Mr. Wood sees."

Monte's knee-jerk charming smile quickly disappeared as a painfully cringey feeling came over him. It was a sharp pain he felt deep in the lining of his stomach that made him think again about his recent poor choices. This feeling was regret.

"Yes, ma'am," Monte said with his head hanging.

"Uh-uh," Nurse Petty corrected, lifting Monte's chin with her index knuckle and commanding gently, "always keep your head up in life, just like the King we see you as, baby."

25

GREED

THE CLASS WAS SILENT. Monte's eyes immediately found Mr. Wood's as he entered classroom 32. Everyone appeared as though they were engrossed in their books at their desks, but their raised eyebrows said otherwise as Monte snaked through the groups of desks and chairs.

Monte avoided Nathalie's gaze as her eyes followed his path back to his desk.

"I thought for sure you were a goner," Bao said, leaning over to whisper.

Monte shook his head.

"I thought they were going to clean out your desk or something."

"They just might," Monte whispered back.

"Yeah?" Bao replied, losing his place within his reading. "I saw your mom through the window as I was throwing away my lunch. She was walking towards the front office. Tell me you didn't have a midday parent-teacher conference!"

"Mr. Bulvarian!" Mr. Wood shouted. "Is a conference needed with your mother, as well?"

"No, sir," Bao said hurriedly.

"I'll tell you about it after school," Monte said without moving his lips.

"I can't. I've gotta walk my little sis to parent pickup. She's got a dentist appointment. We'll catch up at the hayride – if you're still alive."

Monte gulped, nearly swallowing his tongue. "Yeah, I'll probably just head out as soon as Mr. Wood dismisses us anyway. I want to check on something at the corner store."

"Oh, yeah?" Bao replied with what almost passed for disinterest.

He squinted his eyes from behind his frames, but he could see perfectly.

The hallways were chaotic as students traversed in opposite directions. There were no orderly lines or students walking with fingers over their mouths one after the other. The final bell had rung, and the only students that remained in the building were after-school care kids and volunteers for the Fall Festival.

"Excuse me," Bao said, splitting two first-grade siblings running towards parent pick-up. "And slow down, too! This isn't a highway, you know."

Bao was making his way to the kinder side of the school to pick up his little sister as Ms. Bulvarian waited patiently outside. The daily duties of being a big brother, as she would always say to her son.

As much as it pained Bao to pull away from a good book, deep down, he was proud to be there for his little sister. As a baby, her first words weren't Dada or Mama; they were Bao Bao.

At nine years old, Bao knew he was the only father-figure in her immediate life, and he took it upon himself to always protect and be there for her.

As Bao approached the laminated stop sign taped to the corner of a hallway intersection, he spotted Gus peeking into the window of Mrs. Heart-Moore's office. He stood there for a moment as he put his hands into his pants pockets and rocked on the heels of his feet. His eyes narrowed as he watched Gus's rounded knuckles tap on the glass to confirm no one was there.

Unaware he had company, Gus continued to peer through the nearly closed blinds of the dimly lit counselor's office until he caught the reflection of Monte's best friend in the window.

"I don't think anyone's in there," Bao said loudly, announcing his presence.

Gus didn't respond as he checked the handle to see if it was secured.

Waiting for his chance to cross the bustling hallway, Bao watched as Gus slowly turned the knob to slip into the vacant office. Immediately, he cut in between students heading to after-school care and reached to close Miss Heart-Moore's door.

"What do you think you're doing?" Bao interrogated, wrinkling his nose. "Can't you see no one's in there?"

"Mind your business," Gus said, wiping the German chocolate remnants from the corners of his mouth.

"This doesn't have anything to do with you, book boy."

"You taking Monte's Tiger's Eye has everything to do with me, though" Bao paused. "Didn't think I saw you do that earlier this morning, huh."

Gus stopped and turned to look at Bao but avoided eye contact. "I don't know what you're talking about."

"You know exactly what I mean, thief," Bao accused. "He's been looking all over for it, and I don't think he's gonna be happy when he finds you."

"Please, Bao, I don't want to give back the stone," Gus said sorrowfully as he overpowered Bao, twisting the knob and forcing the door back open. "I need it. It's *mine* now."

Adjusting his now-crooked glasses, Bao squinted into the doorway and saw the Fall Festival carnival tickets rolled into a wheel atop Mrs. Heart-Moore's desk.

Slamming the door this time, Bao's efforts at making a scene were pointless as after-school banter and commotion had overtaken the hallways.

"Tell me you're not about to do what I think you're about to do?!" Bao pressed.

Gus's drooping eyelids fell even lower as he stared back at Bao, expressionless.

"That's not cool, man," Bao said with disappointment in his voice. "Those tickets are for the kids who can't afford to buy tickets of their own — that's stealing."

Gus raised and lowered his shoulders in one motion and opened his mouth to let out a whisper. "I can't afford to buy them either."

"So settle for the one she'll give you with the rest of us!"

"Nah," Gus said, blockading the doorway with his weight and slipping into Mrs. Heart-Moore's office. "I need more than one ticket—"

"Bao Baooo!"

As Bao fought against Gus's massive frame, a voice caught his attention.

Losing focus for one moment, Bao somehow allowed Gus to wedge past his planted foot and close the door behind him.

"Is Miss Heart-Moore in there, Bao Bao?"

"No," Bao said, twisting the now-locked doorknob. "A thief is in there!"

"A thief, Bao Bao?" his little sister replied, confused and afraid.

"Yes, Star," Bao said, banging on the door. "Come outta there!"

"I wanna go to Mommy, Bao Bao," she said, beginning to cry. "I'm scared."

Bao stopped knocking.

He took one last look through the blinds and watched Gus stuffing his pockets with tickets. He looked down to waist height and saw two tears fall down the face of his kid sister.

"Come on, Star," he said soothingly, picking her up. "He just needs the help he deserves."

Star placed her head on her big brother's shoulder as he hoisted her up and carried her to parent pick-up. "I love you, Bao Bao."

"I love you more."

26

THE SEARCH CONTINUES

MONTE WALKED with a purpose as he clutched the plastic buckles of his Jansport backpack, ignoring his scraped knee and elbows. He walked in a perfectly straight line as one foot stepped exactly in front of the other in the opposite direction of the school grounds.

The sidewalk that lined the affordable-housing complexes and many condemned homes was uneven and signaled the presence of the Southside neighborhood beyond Three Pyramids Elementary. Tree roots had begun to crack the cement as they grew. Weeks-old potato chip bags blew on the ground, and the smell of someone frying catfish escaped a nearby screen door.

The space between the steps of homes and the street frustrated Monte. His eyes bounced from a line-drive stare to bending around the beginning of each home's front yard. Some yards had lush green grass that homeowners took extreme care of with a watchful eye over their yards, while many others weren't much of a yard at all and served as a holding tank for a wild animal — like Big Luther.

Some front yards were parking lots for cars that no longer started. The grass that had once thrived was now stones and dirt. Weeds as tall as cornstalks hid the broken blinds and windows of condemned homes.

Monte felt the eyes of squatters as he walked past them, one foot after the other, with one thing on his mind. Refusing to allow others' thoughts to slow his thinking, Monte marched on to the corner store.

Just great, Monte thought as he elbowed the crosswalk button at the intersection. Lifting his jean-jacket hood, he slowed down and waited for the fourth graders behind him to catch up to blend in.

The blood that stained Monte's denim had dried but not before trickling down to his ankle and staining his crisp white sneakers. With so many lies to keep up with and people let down, his new sneakers were the last thing on his mind, though. It had all been downhill after countless kids kept kicking the back of his shoes during the fire drill earlier, and he knew it.

As usual around this time of day, the line to get in the cornerstone was wrapped around the building.

Yeah, I'm not waiting in that, Monte thought to himself avoiding eye contact while his eyes scanned the side-walk leading to the gravel parking lot.

Monte hoped by some chance Gus had dropped his Tiger's Eye before he had gotten far. Coupled with the homeless people and gangs that frequented the corner store, though, Monte knew the odds of him finding his Tiger's Eye still on the ground was slim. He knew the way the sun caught it in the light was sure to catch someone's eye and could be pawned for a couple of dollars at 24hr Pawn Shop in the district. He didn't care, though; he was going to try before putting his pride aside and admitting to his best friend he'd lost yet another prized possession in his life.

Shards of shattered glass glistened as they lay wedged in between the cracked concrete. The way the sun hit at certain angles refracted the light, making it impossible to spot the quartz.

He recounted the moments before and after the collision and even walked to the corner where he'd hopped over the sofa seat cushions and broken high chair.

Not there, either. Monte exhaled, eyeing the speeding city bus pass by him by with an ad that read Keep Going plastered on the side of it.

Just above the poster, Monte caught a glimpse of his reflection in the tinted windows. He wasn't sure, but he thought there were figures nodding behind the smudged handprints of the black glass — figures that Monte had seen growing up as a child and just recently while being bandaged. In that moment, he heard their soft hymns spill from their soulful recollections of joy and pain — fear and faith. He smelled the cocoa butter and incense ashes that were currently being masked by the exhaust of public transportation.

Huh? Monte questioned himself.

The bus was moving so fast that he couldn't tell if the figures were on board or not. In his reflection they seemed to hover over him, angelic in a sense, while looking over both of his shoulders. Quickly, he turned around, thinking two people were sneaking up to surprise him — and not in a good way.

Seeing no one and turning back around quickly, Monte came to the realization that both the Tiger's Eye and city bus were gone.

27

WATCHFUL EYES

LIKE A CAT, Monte crept his way to the front of the corner store line. He timed it just right to be able to catch the doorman allowing the next five kids in.

"Papiiii," Monte said slyly. "I think I left something really important this morning; can I come inside to ask the owner's son right quick?"

Papi wielded his day-old toothpick like a sword between his chapped lips. "You tryin' to play me to cut the line, Monte?"

"Not even," Monte replied patting his pockets. "I spent all of my money here this morning. I just gotta ask Paco something for my peace of mind."

Papi looked around at the neighborhood kids who were all waiting pseudo-patiently for their own turn to enter the corner store and whispered, "Now, you know that's going to start a riot out here, Monte."

"I knooow, but my mom is going to start a riot at home if I don't get back what I lost. Just let me in to ask Paco really quickly. I'm not even going to buy anything."

Papi knew Monte was a good kid who came from a good family. He'd seen his father and Mark frequent the store often growing up.

"Make it quick, Monte, and you'd better not buy anything," Papi said loudly, winking at Monte.

Monte nodded in appreciation as Papi resumed the order of the line outside. Kids resented Monte's successful cut and loudly let Papi know it.

"Yo, what's up, Paco?!" Monte said as he stood next to another kid buying something lemony and an ice-cold Mrs. Peach soda. "You wouldn't happen to have a lost and found, would ya?"

"That'll be $2.50," Paco said to the kid in line, then laughed. "A lost and found? You hear this guy?"

Dejected, Monte reframed his question and replied, "I'm looking for something that either I lost here or was stolen. Anyone turned anything in?"

"Ahh, you lost something, you say?" Paco questioned, oddly interested as he took three dollar bills from the boy. "Is this something nice, by chance?"

Monte raised an eyebrow. "It's mine, so that doesn't even matter."

Paco slammed two quarters on the counter and slid them across from him. He clenched his teeth and spat, "Whatever it is, it's probably at the pawnshop by now."

"What about the security tapes outside? Don't those work?"

"You got a lawyer or something?" Paco said, wary of Monte's line of questioning. "Matter of fact, are you buying something or no, papa — you're holding up my money from outside."

Monte flashed an ice-cold Mrs. Peach of his own and placed his exact change on the counter, glaring at Paco. There was nothing he could do other than pay for his soda and ignore Paco's stubbornness.

This is getting me nowhere, he thought.

"Thanks for nothing," Monte curled his lip and spat, "and you mean your pops' money, too — you just work here."

Papi chuckled to himself at Monte's quick-witted remark from the door. He had a strong disdain for the owner's son, too, as he had watched Paco talk down to kids over the years.

"Nice one," he whispered to Monte as he reached for the door handle. "One day he's going to try the wrong kid. I'm not even going to say anything about that soda you weren't supposed to buy."

Monte smirked and winked back at Papi as he reached for his backpack to conceal his Mrs. Peach from the line of kids still waiting outside.

"Thanks again, Papi."

"Any time," he replied. "Hope you find whatever it is you're looking for."

A few kids had left the long line and moved on to settle for whatever was at their homes. Some had gone a few streets over for quarter freeze cups from Mrs. Johnson.

In normal fashion, Monte headed in the opposite direction of the crowd as he dragged his feet through the rocks that led to the gravel parking lot.

Swinging his backpack from his shoulder, he reached for the one thing that hadn't gotten him in trouble that day. The one thing that would work toward making him happy, he believed.

The sweat from the cold can made his palm slick, and Monte gripped it as if someone was trying to take it from him.

The way the condensation and aluminum glistened in the early-evening sun made Monte think of the Tiger's Eye.

He thought of all of the poor decisions he had made since losing the stone and of the forgiveness he was still searching for in others.

"I gotta do better," Monte said quietly as he brought the can to his lips.

"As do we all, soldier," a voice from behind Monte said commandingly.

Monte neither responded nor turned around as he welcomed the carbonated beverage meeting his taste buds.

"Have you found what you've been in search of?" the homeless man said to Monte.

"I don't know what you're talking about," Monte finally turned then paused, reading the patch of his last name on his tattered black and green army fatigue vest, "Campbell—"

"That's Staff Sergeant Campbell to you, private," the war veteran corrected.

Monte laughed to himself and took another gulp of his Mrs. Peach.

"I saw what happened to the stone this morning."

Nearly spitting out his soda, Monte looked at the fatigues-clad man.

He looked at the fold of his bucket hat and how it draped over the right side of his reflective aviator sunglasses.

The tank top he wore underneath his vest, which had once been a uniform jacket with sleeves, had been white long ago but now was stained with earthy tones and a smell of yesterday.

"You were there this morning?" Monte questioned, raising an eyebrow. "Yeah, that's right, you were barking at someone on your walkie talkie between the cars over there."

"It's not a walkie talkie, it's a command device."

Monte rudely laughed to himself as he conceded, "Whatever you say, bro."

"And if you must know, I was receiving commands from my sergeant general about a top-secret mission that I can't tell you about," Staff Sergeant Campbell replied, looking over his shoulder. "Sometimes my signal is weak and communication goes out."

Monte took a sip of his Mrs. Peach and responded through closed lips, "Mmhmm."

He allowed an awkward silence to give the veteran a chance to tell him what he had seen, but instead the man just stood and adjusted the tarnished hanging stars and medals.

"So…" Monte replied impatiently. "Did you see Gus take it or not?"

"Is Gus the enemy?"

"Duh!" Monte replied without thinking. "Well, I don't want to say he's an enemy," he backpedaled. "I just think he took something of mine, and I want it back."

"I see," Staff Sergeant Campbell said, deeply concerned. "You know, a soldier with a chip on his shoulder is a dangerous man."

"I guess, bro," Monte said, immaturely overlooking the message. "So did he take it or not?"

Staff Sergeant Campbell chuckled to himself as he reached for his command device to check if it was still there.

"If Gus is the husky kid who pocketed the stone after you two collided, then yes, he picked it up."

"I knew it!" Monte shouted. "I've been looking for him all day!"

"Maybe he needs it?" Staff Sergeant Campbell suggested.

"Needs it?" Monte spat. "He needs to *give it back* — that's what he needs."

"You ever had something that gave you strength?" Staff Sergeant Campbell quizzed. "Something that gave you a reason to enjoy life?"

Monte reached for jacket pockets as he broke eye contact.

"I saw him marveling at the stone in an apartment he squats in over at Shady 8's."

"Shady 8's!?" Monte challenged the man. "That place has been boarded up for years and has a fence that's ten feet high. Nobody's in there."

"You know, I used to lead soldiers like you — soldiers who don't listen."

Monte dismissed Staff Sergeant Campbell's made-up war stories and questioned, "Isn't there barbed wire at the top of those fences?"

"Only criminals hop fences," Staff Sergeant Campbell retorted.

Monte disagreed but realized he was going back and forth with a stranger for no reason.

"Ok, ok, ok," Monte said. "So it sounds as though you not only know a way in but also know where he hides out?"

"Affirmative."

"Sooooo, let's go," Monte insisted.

Staff Sergeant Campbell reached for his command device to ensure it wasn't picking up on their conversation. "I don't know, I'm on strict orders at the moment, and I've got to be ready when they call."

Monte shook his head and discarded his soda can in an overflowing trash can.

"I'm Monte, by the way," he said, keeping a smell's distance away from his new companion as they walked towards Shady 8's.

"No need for introductions, soldier. I know who you are."

28

NO TRESPASSING

LOOKING over his shoulder without fully turning his head, Staff Sergeant Campbell crossed the pothole-riddled street and led Monte to an opening that had been concealed by the brush of bushes and broken tree branches.

"The entrance is right there," the man said as he peered through the fence at the boarded-up windows and littered parking lot. "You've got it from here, private. I've got a rendezvous with Bravo back at base."

"What?!" Monte scoffed as an inkling of fear began to set in. "Bravo is going to have wait, man." Monte turned and looked at Campbell. "I'm not going in there by myself!"

Campbell only shrugged.

"Man, you're definitely coming in there with me —
I'm not *that* big and bad now."

"You are not my staff sergeant, corporal!"

Monte's face paled.

"This is enemy territory and not a mission."

"This is a mission, Staff Sergeant Campbell!" Monte
said, turning sideways and ducking through the gap
in the fence. "This is a rescue mission."

"You're not understanding, private," Campbell said,
kneeling down and lowering his aviator sunglasses.
"Kids go in there and don't come out."

Monte contemplated the risks of trespassing on the
condemned property. He thought of the white vans
that were said to pull up to children at the sandbox
by the volleyball courts and take them away forever.
The possibility of being kidnapped and never seeing
his family again was scary. Still, Monte was bent on
finding Gus.

"I don't believe those stories, bro," Monte said,
emotionless, peering through the holes in the fence.

"Come on, man," he continued with a hint of
pleading in his voice. "What happened to never leave

a man behind, because that's certainly what you're doing now."

Behind Staff Sergeant Campbell's reflective lenses, his eyes widened at the thought of the dangers that loomed in Shady 8's for him, as well — children weren't the only people who disappeared without a trace.

Staff Sergeant Campbell became confused and conflicted as he backed away from the fence that divided them.

"C'mon, bro…" Monte pleaded, taking one last shot at pressuring him. "Don't leave me."

Staff Sergeant Campbell stopped in his tracks. The words 'don't leave me' triggered a memory from the battlefield where he had once abandoned his platoon, resulting in his AWOL status and dismissal from the army. He had led them into battle but had run for the hills the moment the first shots were fired. At the end of the war, fellow staff sergeants had found Campbell in a barn with sheep. Ever since, the man's life had spiraled downward without any support.

"Hellooo?" Monte said, ready to give up. "I thought you were here to maintain my development as a soldier; to bring me up in the ranks and be all I can be?"

Suddenly grinning, Staff Sergeant Campbell snapped back into the present. "I knew you had it in you, Monte; I'll make you the best second lieutenant yet."

Monte smiled, just happy to not have to trespass on the abandoned property alone.

"But first," Staff Sergeant Campbell said excitedly, "I've gotta radio this is in to the sergeant major!"

29

TRESPASSING

"I THOUGHT you said he squatted in Building 5," Monte said as he looked up at Building S.

"Look closer, soldier," Staff Sergeant Campbell said, pointing at the misleading information hanging from its loose screw. "It's holding on for dear life."

Monte strained his eyes while stepping over years-old grocery store coupons.

It was hard to see as their shadows grew longer the further they walked into the dimly sunlit hallway. A mouse scurried in fear as Monte dragged his feet over an old pizza box.

"This is it," Staff Sergeant Campbell said, stepping aside from a doorway.

Monte shuffled his feet directly in front of the looming door and eyed the peeling deep red paint. He looked at the keyhole as if he could unlock the deadbolt with his mind and scanned the rusted doorknob. He thought of reaching out to see if it open, but instead he hesitated.

Looking down at his feet, Monte's eyes caught the black and yellow handle of a destroyed screwdriver. Lifting it from atop the classified section of an outdated newspaper, he looked at Staff Sergeant Campbell then back at the door.

"Looks like a key," Monte stated.

"A broken key to me, if you're asking."

Monte tossed the useless tool and lifted his knuckles to the faded door.

His heart began to race with the uncertainty of who was on the other side.

"Well?" Staff Sergeant Campbell whispered.

"Shh," Monte said as he knocked twice.

Before Monte could bring his hands back to his sides, the door creaked open.

"It was never locked," Monte said.

"So!" Staff Sergeant Campbell scoffed. "I'm not going in there."

"Stop being afraid and let's just peek in to see if the stone is here," Monte pushed as he stepped into the apartment.

"Hellooo," Monte called out. "Gus, you in here?"

"I really think we should get outta here," Staff Sergeant Campbell said as he eyed broken toy soldiers that lay near a sink filled with dirty dishes.

"Check out these old comics near this broken recliner."

"Are these anti-hero comics?" Staff Sergeant Campbell said, quickly identifying them while thinking back to his childhood. "Soldiers used to hoot and holler over the scams Jarod the Fraud would pull off in these stories."

Monte shook his head as he flipped through the pages of *Jarod The Fraud*. He despised a thief and had never found an interest in this anti-hero.

"I remember one story where he pretended to be the mailman and stole people's packages from their front porches."

Monte tuned Staff Sergeant Campbell out as he scanned the room, finding nothing but corner-store and frozen-food wrappers.

"I think you might be outta luck, soldier."

"Luck?" Monte shot back, cutting his eyes at the man. "What's that?"

Just as he was about to give up, something in the crevices of the recliner caught Monte's eye.

Like an iceberg, only the tip of the object was visible between the torn seat cushions. It twinkled as the setting sun cast orange light through broken blinds.

"And then there was another time where Jarod the Fraud—"

"Stop telling me about the thief, bro," Monte said cutting into another con-story from the comic book. "Something's in this chair."

"As you reach to take something that's not yours?"

"Be quiet," Monte snapped. "It might be my Tiger's Eye."

Digging into the folds of the chair, Monte felt the grittiness of years-old crumbs scraping against his fingers, a few of them getting wedged under his nails.

Feeling past old buttons and a marble or two, he found a solid object. *It's cold,* Monte thought.

Tugging at the object, he tried to free it from the leaning recliner.

"It's stuck!" Monte said as he struggled in frustration. "It must be hooked on something."

"Maybe that means you should leave it alone."

"I almost got it, though."

"Wait," Staff Sergeant Campbell said, holding his breath and raising a finger. "I heard something."

Monte shifted his eyes as the man reached for his command device.

Hearing nothing, Monte bent closer and analyzed the cold metal that peeked from the furniture bound by string.

"It looks like a locket," Monte said, confused. "It doesn't open, though..."

Turning it over, Monte found an engraving and read it out loud.

"To our special boy, Augustus Coogely. We'll always love you forever and ever. Mom and Dad."

"You think they're—"

"I don't know, Staff Sergeant," Monte interrupted. "But I'm sure he lost it in this broken chair."

Just then, tires screeched outside of the building as static could be heard coming from Staff Sergeant Campbell's command device. His eyes beamed at Monte. Someone was trying to come through the static.

"Is that your walkie talkie going off?!" Monte asked incredulously.

"Staff Sergeant Campbell," the voice became clearer as Campbell switched channels, "this is the command base, do you read us, over?"

Monte's eyes widened as the tires screeched louder in the background.

"Get outta there, staff sergeant!" The voice became clearer through the static. "The white vans have arrived. I repeat. The white vans have arrived! Over."

Through the broken blinds, Monte saw the tops of white vans barreling through the parking lot.

Monte tugged at the silver locket with all of his might, freeing it from the chair as Staff Sergeant Campbell yelled, "Abort! Abort!" while breaking for the door.

"Don't leave me, Staff Sergeant Campbell!" Monte hollered, pocketing the silver locket as he slipped on some coupon clippings just outside the door.

This time, Monte's plea had no effect. Staff Sergeant Campbell was long gone in search of safety—or maybe sheep. Missing which direction his accomplice went in, Monte guessed incorrectly and ran to the opposite side from where the two had come in.

He's gone, Monte determined, peeking from a back hall.

Hearing the doors of the vans opening and shutting, Monte dashed from Building 5 to a neighboring one just beyond the volleyball courts.

Just gotta make it to that wall, Monte coached himself, fueling his mental strength.

"Hey, kid!" a man in a pinstripe button-down shirt shouted. "What're you doing here!?"

Monte didn't hear a single word as he ran at top speed toward a stone wall. *They're coming for me!* Monte thought.

By now Monte was at a full sprint. Leading with his right foot, he sprung himself up while hitting the old stone wall with a thud.

Adjusting his backpack, he swept his feet over the top barrier and landed like a cat on the other side.

Man, that was close, he thought, exhaling as he bent over to place his hands on his knees.

Monte wasn't out of the woods yet, however.

Rusted chains scraped the concrete in the distance of the massive yard Monte had landed in. It looked familiar. He recognized the fence facing the street and the car in the driveway he could just see around the house.

The sound of chains was soon coupled with a growl that grew more distinct, coming from a trash shelter of cardboard boxes.

Monte swallowed hard as he saw the bricks lining the bottom of the fence he knew he would have to sprint to make it to. The chains and the growl grew louder.

Monte crept quietly as far away from the entry to the ramshackle doghouse as he could. The dry fall leaves crunched as his sneakers met them.

Stepping over a rag doll that had been gnawed to tatters, Monte picked up his pace, holding his breath in an attempt not to make a sound.

Friendlier metal chains could be heard in the distance as the twins pulled up, nearly passing the house on their bikes.

"Yo, Monte!" Darren yelled, cupping his mouth. "What're you doing in Big Luther's yard?!"

"Get outta there!" Dave yelled. "Run!"

The growls turned into barks as Big Luther appeared, drooling, from the shadows.

Monte froze in fear as the beast, feared even by other dogs, looked at Monte like lunchmeat.

"Run!!!!" Darren cried out as Monte bolted for the fence.

Straining against his heavy chain, Big Luther leapt from the grocery store boxes that made up his makeshift doghouse and ran for his next meal.

While dodging old bones from animals that had mistakenly fallen into the wrong yard, just as Monte had, and stepping over Big Luther's droppings, Monte was almost to the fence.

"Run faster, Monte!" Darren cried out. "He's right behind you!"

"He's not gonna make it," Dave lamented.

Feeling the drool fling onto the back of his forearms, Monte knew Big Luther was in biting distance.

As he leapt for the fence, there was a loud whimper as the iron chain snatched Big Luther from his pursuit, yanking him back. Defeated, Big Luther ran with his tail between his legs back into the darkness of his cardboard boxes.

"Yeah! More like Little Luther!" David shot at the canine bully.

Darren rolled his eyes at his twin brother as Monte landed on their side of the fence and fell to his knees. His favorite shirt was torn, his Tiger's Eye was gone, and he had nearly been mauled by Big Luther.

"You ok, bro?" Darren asked, concerned.

"I'm good," Monte said while raising his index finger, closing his eyes and heaving for breath. "Staff Sergeant Campbell's command device really does work."

30

WE'RE ALL KINGS

DISHES WERE PILED high in murky water in the dimly lit kitchen at the twins' house.

The trash can beneath the light switch in the doorway was beginning to overflow as paper plates and brown fast-food wrappers balanced atop one another.

The countertops were gritty, and Monte reconsidered placing his hands on them as he watched David raid the pantry for an after-school snack. *Eh, maybe not,* he thought, folding his arms and placing his hands in his armpits.

"Chips? Nah. Snack cakes? Nope…"

Monte shook his head as he turned his attention to Darren, who was reading a note held to the fridge with a magnet. There was money attached that Monte saw the older brother slide into his pocket.

"Mom left a note, bro."

"Yeah?" David replied with a mouthful of salted butter crackers. "What does it say?"

"She has to work a double tonight, as usual."

"What's new?" David sighed, blowing crumbs onto the countertop.

"Ew." Monte cringed, clearing his throat and shifting his eyes to Darren's pocket, where the money was concealed.

"Oh, she left us $10, too, for food tonight at the hayride," Darren said, pulling out the crinkled bill. "She also said for you to do the dishes and take out the trash, lil' bro. C'mon, Sheriff Monte, I've got just the shirt for you in my room."

Darren hurriedly discarded the note onto the counter and disappeared into the hallway.

"I hope it's clean," Monte muttered, picking up the note that gave instructions to clean a little differently:

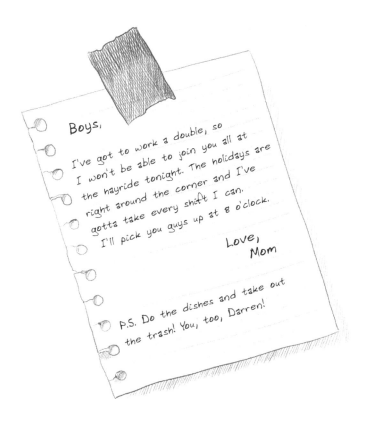

Boys,

I've got to work a double, so I won't be able to join you all at the hayride tonight. The holidays are right around the corner and I've gotta take every shift I can. I'll pick you guys up at 8 o'clock.

Love,
Mom

P.S. Do the dishes and take out the trash! You, too, Darren!

The hallway was long and littered with piles of clothes that were separated into piles of denim and delicates.

A pile of towels and a pile of linens were connected by crew socks and extension cords that lay throughout the hallway.

Stepping over the dirty laundry, Monte entered Darren's doorway and leaned on the frame.

"I've been wanting to give you this shirt for a while," Darren said, standing on his tiptoes to reach the top shelf of his closet. "I got it for taking a survey at the mall, and it always makes me think of you when I see it, searching for something else."

Monte smiled, reaching out for the jet-black T-shirt that bore a tilted golden crown.

"I thought it would be more fitting if you had it, honors boy."

"Psh, c'mon now." Monte held it out with both hands. "I don't have any money for it, now."

Darren laughed. "Never, bro. That's from me to you."

"What's funny back here?" David said, barging into the room and conversation, feeling left out.

"I see you found another snack," Monte said, eyeing the bowl of peanut butter and chocolate puffed cereal.

"I see you found my soon-to-be T-shirt!"

Monte and Darren looked at one another wide-eyed, unable to tell whether David was seriously upset or not.

The look on his face told two stories as he spooned another heap of cereal into his mouth.

"Bro, I wanted that shirt," David whined. "Monte, I got this motorcycle shirt you'd probably like?"

"Nah," Monte whispered, entranced by the metallic gold that shone in the bedroom light. "This might be my new favorite shirt."

"C'mon, couldn't we have just swung by your house if you really needed a shirt?"

"And risk my dad seeing me and bringing up earlier today? I'd never make it out to the hayride."

"That is true, bro," Darren chimed in.

"I wanna be a king, too, though," David said, dropping the empty bowl to his side.

"We're all young kings, bro," Monte said, changing shirts. "Each and every one of us from this Southside neighborhood, whether we're in the honors program or not."

Darren nodded slowly.

"C'mon, y'all. I'll help out with the dishes, so we can go."

"We've gotta lock our bikes up, Monte," Darren said, applying his brakes. "You want us to drop you off at the front over there by parent pick-up?"

Holding onto the handlebars tightly, Monte recognized the van that's typically parked across the street from the twins' house and said, "Yeah, that's cool. There's Bao getting dropped off over there."

"Yo, Bao!" Monte shouted, hopping off of Darren's bike and adjusting to being back on two feet. "We'll catch up with you guys inside, bros."

Popping wheelies, both Darren and David pedaled toward the bike cage for safekeeping.

"Hey, Ms. Bulvarian!" Monte said, ducking his head into the passenger-seat window. "Thank you for letting Bao come to the hayride tonight. It's going to be a really great time."

"Oh, I'm certain it will, young Monte," Ms. Bulvarian said, gripping the steering wheel tightly, thinking back to her recent call from their teacher. "I heard your mother came to the school earlier today."

"Yes, ma'am," Monte replied, cutting his eyes at Bao, who sat bolt upright, staring directly through the windshield.

"I've seen beautiful things come about from my Bao baby since he's met you, Monte. He's outspoken, like you. Fearless, like you, and a leader, like you. You've taught him to be so many great things as I'm certain he has for you—"

"Bao baby!" Star shouted from her car seat in the rear as Bao adjusted his lime green glasses. "C'mon, Ma."

Ms. Bulvarian loosened her grip from the steering wheel and sighed as she smiled warmly at both boys. "Be great, Monte, and you, too, Bao baby."

31

RUNNING YELLOW LIGHTS

"NOW, I know you're used to college parties, Regina, but you're going to love my old elementary school's hayride—"

"I've never been to a hayride festival. Is it like a carnival?" Regina replied, applying her black eyeliner in the flip-down passenger mirror.

"Kinda sorta."

"There'll be music and food, right?" Regina said, batting her eyelashes.

"Mmhmm," Mark said, turning the dial to his radio up. "Plenty of it."

"Sounds like a carnival to me, Marcus."

Mark smirked, bobbing his head to the upbeat music. Speeding up to beat the light, he changed lanes without signaling, nearly causing Regina to mess up her makeup.

"Whoops!" Mark said, swerving to the left. "There was a pothole back there."

"You almost made me mess up!" Regina shouted. "You're so annoying."

Mark's charming smile grew larger as he shrugged in a half-hearted apology.

"Well, since you know carnivals so much," Mark paused to release the clutch and shift gears, "what's your favorite ride?"

Regina waited for the next song to transition as she grabbed on to Mark's soft leather seat cushions. She checked her seatbelt as the car accelerated, weaving in and out of traffic.

"The Ferris wheel because it goes slow, Marcus," Regina said, checking her makeup once more in the side mirror and seeing tire marks and smoke in the distance. "You know I hate it when you drive fast."

"Well, good thing we're not going fast!" Mark shouted, smiling and mashing the gas pedal, pushing his car even harder.

The gauges all moved as gasoline combusted inside of the engine. With every stab at the gas, exhaust filled the muffler, releasing the car's emissions into the air behind them.

Tires screeched and rubber burned as people gawked at Mark and Regina escaping their personal cloud of smoke. One boy pointed, nudging another to see what was coming before it was gone.

"Who is he racing?"

"I don't know, but I wish it was me," his companion replied.

Releasing the gas pedal slowly, Mark did not apply the brakes. He allowed the weight of the car to slow its momentum on its own as he anticipated their upcoming turn.

"You see that corner store right there?"

"Ew," Regina rejected. "They actually sell food there?"

"Chill…" Mark said, laughing while shrugging off his girlfriend's insult. "The owner's son used to short-change people and get away with it. It only took one time and it never happened to me again."

Regina sucked her teeth. "Get outta here. No one's stealing from these kids and the community out here."

Mark hit a hard left the moment there was a gap in oncoming traffic. "I'm for real." Mark began to laugh. "I got home and realized I was cheated out of two dollars and marched right back to that store."

"No you didn't!"

"I did!" Mark said, smiling. "It's funny now, but it wasn't funny back then."

"Speaking of *cheating*," Regina said, pivoting the conversation. "I hope you didn't let that boy cheat off of your midterm test earlier today?"

"Ha! Who, Caesar?" Mark forced another laugh to give the impression he had forgotten. "He tried it, but I had to turn him down. I work too hard in that garage for that scholarship, and to risk it all for that guy? Get outta here."

Regina didn't reply as the lights from the Ferris wheel had caught her attention. There were kids everywhere and, as expected, no place to park.

"How did they get this huge Ferris wheel on this tiny elementary P.E. field?"

"Hey now!" Mark interjected. "It only looks like a teeny tiny space because of all of the booths."

"I guess," Regina replied with doubt in her voice.

"Monte got in trouble today in school, by the way."

"Stop it," Regina said with sarcasm. "I don't believe it."

"Everything I say is a fib, huh?" Mark said under his breath.

"I beg your pardon?"

"I said, 'My mom was really upset. She went to the school today and all.'"

Regina remained silent, having heard what Mark said under his breath but allowing him to finish spilling the tea.

"You gotta promise not to bring it up because I don't think she told our dad about it."

Regina rolled her eyes.

"I'm just saying," Mark pleaded, approaching just enough pavement to park. "For real, she called me earlier after the exam."

"Boy!" Regina retorted. "You know I stay quiet—"

"Not in the car you don't," Mark interrupted.

"That's different," she said, shifting her weight in her seat. "It's just me and you in here. Plus, your mama is mean. I hear her when you two are on the phone."

"She's just protective," Mark consoled, placing his hand on Regina's knee. "Anyway, Monte busted a kid's nose wide open with a basketball today. There was blood everywhere, Mom told me."

"Get outta here," Regina groaned, shaking her head. "What're you going to say to him when you see him?"

Cutting the wheel, Mark backed into the slim space between two cars. He detached the radio display from his car and tucked it under his seat. "I have no clue, babe. But I told you the hayride was going to be a great time, and that's exactly what we're going to have."

"Mmhmm… What are we going to do first?" Regina replied, unbuckling her seatbelt and smiling with the Ferris wheel lights in her eyes.

"Find my little brother."

32

COME ONE, COME ALL

THE SMELL of caramel kettle-cooked popcorn and roasted corn lingered in the air as it blew in the fall night. Entrance was free for the entire community, but tickets were needed to play the games and eat until you could eat no more.

The Fall Festival was Three Pyramids' biggest fundraiser. The money made by the carnival games and hayride paid for the winter choir concert, new recess equipment, and even standardized test prep for all kids in the spring.

"You want to eat first, bro?" Monte suggested, leading the way. "They didn't have anything to eat at the twins' house."

"I don't believe it," Bao rejected. "David has a snack every time I see him; he eats nonstop."

Both boys laughed as they made their way toward the funnel cake booth.

"Yo, Monte! Bao, wait up!" the twins yelled, racing through the crowd of students and parents.

"What's up, Bao?" Darren asked, nearly out of breath. "You owe me two dollars, little bro."

"Psh... I beat *you* here!" David said with his hands on his hips.

"Heard you got a new bike, Dave," Bao probed. "How's it ride?"

"You can't even feel the pavement underneath you."

"Let's just hope he doesn't lose this one this time," Darren said, flapping his shirt for air.

"I didn't lose the last one," David remarked, not holding back. "It was stolen from me."

Darren rolled his eyes as the cashier called for Monte.

"Next in line."

"One funnel cake with extra whipped cream and strawberry topping, please."

"You're gonna be sick," Bao said, turning to the counter. "You know that hayride is going to be a rough ride."

"It'll be worth it," Monte said, eyeing the cashier spooning strawberry preserves from a mason jar. "Some people also call them elephant ears. Have you ever even had one of these, my guy?"

"It just looks like fried dough with powdered sugar on top, Monte."

"Well, I certainly see you're getting what you're paying for with those specs."

"Ha, ha," Bao said, deadpan. "But if that's your way of offering me some, then I'd be more than happy to indulge."

"Can I have a piece, too, Monte?" asked David hopefully.

Monte laughed, turning back to the cashier. "May I have a few more forks for my friends, please?"

33

A NEW FRIEND

"HE'S NOT GONNA DO anything, y'all!" one kid in the crowd gathered around Gus. "He's what my uncle calls a gentle giant."

"A big ol' softy!"

"A mama's boy!"

Gus pulled Monte's Tiger's Eye from his pocket and shifted his weight from one knee to the other as he slowly rose from the ground. Looking away from his attackers, he found a running lane in the kids that surrounded him and darted off.

With a baseball in his hand, Monte was elbowed by Darren pointing to where they could see kids huddled together in laughter.

"What's going on?" Bao turned, squinting and pushing his lime-green glasses up his nose. "What's so funny over there?"

"There he is, Monte!" Darren shouted and turned to Bao. "Monte had us looking all over the Southside for him this afternoon!"

"Looking all over the Southside for who? Gus?" Bao quizzed as Monte cocked back his arm to aim for the dunk tank. "That's why you went back to the corner store after school, huh?"

Another miss.

"He has something of mine, Bao, and I'm going to get it back."

"I see." Bao shook his head as the white and red leather baseball rolled slowly back to Monte's newly dirty basketball sneakers.

"I've been looking for him all day," Monte replied, picking up the ball and throwing another miss. "All roads point to him."

Bao rolled his eyes as he shook his head.

"Ha! Maybe your concerned friend with the four eyes has a better chance at hitting the target, Montellous!" The heckler shouted from the collapsible bench. He was dressed as a jester and challenged carnival-goers to hit the target from twenty feet away. "Is there no one else?"

"Forget this clown, y'all," Monte said, motioning toward the hayride ticket booth. "Someone has something of mine, and I'm going to get it back.

Bao looked at the twins as he picked up on no one knowing exactly who had stolen the quartz, or if it was even stolen at all. However, Bao had seen it all unravel from the very beginning and went to get help from Mrs. Heart-Moore, who was nearby pouring salt on her fire-roasted corn.

"Monte, help!" Gus shouted, running toward him. "They're after me."

Stopping in his tracks, Monte saw the mob of kids being led by Jeff and a bandaged Brandon. While no one seemed to have pushed him, Gus took another tumble as he tried desperately to avoid his captors.

"Whoa!" Monte said as Gus rolled to his feet. He scanned the crowd and saw Brandon leading the charge. "I should've known," Monte said, biting his lip and clasping his hands behind his back.

"This has nothing to do with you, but we can make it about you if you want," Brandon said, turning back to the crowd to ensure they had his back.

Monte didn't back down as he helped Gus up.

"Didn't you get enough of trying to bully someone earlier?" Monte said. "I thought I already taught you this lesson."

"Wait. That's the kid who busted you in the nose, Brandon?" a fifth-grader shouted from the crowd.

Another joined in, "I thought you got that from scoring the game-winning layup!"

Brandon cowered a bit. The spotlight had been turned on him yet again, and boy was it hot.

"The only game-winning layups Brandon is going to be scoring are in out-of-school suspension," Mr.

Wood said, cutting into the crowd alongside Brandon's parents. "We let you slide once with attempted bullying, but certainly not twice in one day. Let's go, young man."

"Break it up, break it up!" Mr. Bolt shouted, shooing fourth and fifth graders who had stopped to see what was going on. "There's nothing to see here!"

Gus's knees were still shaking as he stood frazzled and nearly in tears. He was grassy and out of breath from the running and rolling around he had been doing.

"No offense, but for a big guy, you're a tough one to catch up to, Gus."

"You know my name?"

"Of course I know your name," Monte said, reaching his hand out to help brush some grass off of Gus's back. "I also know you have something of mine."

"You do?" Gus mumbled, unsure if Bao had outed him.

"Kinda sorta," Monte said, thinking hard on his next words. This was the moment he had rehearsed in his mind all day. "I mean, I don't *know* you have it. But

I'm pretty sure you do. You were the last person I ran into after I got it."

Gus bowed his head to hide his feelings.

"I've been looking for you all day, and I even went to that creepy Shady 8's place."

"You went to Shady 8's!?" Gus whisper-yelled. "You must really care for that stone, huh?"

"I mean…" Monte began, eyeing all of his friends that surrounded him. "One of my closest friends gave it to me to help me make better choices, and I felt bad for losing it — kind of like how I lose everything else in life."

"I wish I had close friends, Monte," Gus said, gripping the quartz in his pocket. "I wish I was like you."

"Me?" Monte said, shocked. "Man, I make so many mistakes. I'm surprised I even still have friends." Monte laughed, trying to make light of the moment.

"Friends," Gus sighed, slumping his shoulders. "I think I should—"

"Keep the Tiger's Eye, Gus," Monte cut him off. "I think it's just what you need to build your mental strength to be the king I already see you as."

Gus gasped.

"The king we *all* see you as," Bao said as he reappeared with Mrs. Heart-Moore at his side. "Her included."

A lone tear fell from Gus's cheek as Monte closed the boy's palm, and they both knew it was a symbol of a new friendship.

"Be strong, Gus," Monte said, reaching in to give

him a hug. "Don't let them push you around and get the best of you. We're here for you, bro."

"Thank you, Monte," Gus said in his low baritone voice. "I'll never forget your courage to stand up to people."

"Ahh! Speaking of forgetting," Monte said, reaching into his pocket. "I think I found some buried treasure in your recliner."

Gus's eyes shone brighter than ever as a silver locket dangled from Monte's fingers. "How?" Gus said, gasping. "I've been looking for that for years."

"Ew," Monte said. "It's been sat on for that long?"

"My mom and dad gave me this before they passed away in a car accident. I thought it was gone forever along with them."

"I'm sorry to hear that, bro," Monte said, placing his hand in comfort on Gus's still-grassy shoulder.

"It's ok — it's not your fault. Thank you for letting me keep the Tiger's Eye, again."

Monte smiled at Gus's lifted spirits. "Thank you, as well, new friend," Monte said.

Mrs. Driarson shed a tear as she hugged Mark from behind the crowd of kids. He nodded proudly, knowing his little brother, in this moment, had made the right decision.

"Just beautiful, Montellous," Mrs. Heart-Moore said, placing her hands on both of Gus's shoulders to lead him away. "I think I've got it from here. Gus, let's go sit down and talk about how you've been feeling lately. Maybe we can share a funnel cake, on you, with the missing carnival tickets from my office."

"Yes, ma'am."

34

SELFLESSNESS & ACCOUNTABILITY

"I LOVE YOU SO MUCH, SON," Mrs. Driarson said as she held Monte tightly. "That was a very selfless thing you did back there."

"Man, you should have taken that rock back! I taught you better than that, little brother," Mark joked, taking a subtle elbow jab to the kidney from Regina.

"I really felt bad for losing it, Ma," Monte said with regret in his voice. "But I knew that he needed it more than me, and I wanted to do something good for a change. I've been screwing up a lot lately, and I'm not proud of it. I'm sorry for embarrassing you and our family, Mom."

"Baby," Monte's mom said, reaching to hold his hands, "you can never embarrass me. You are my proudest creation."

"Hey!" Mark said, interrupting.

"As long as you always try to make the right choice, your father and I will stand by your decisions until the very end."

"Aww," Regina said, fanning her eyeliner, "y'all are going to make me mess up my makeup."

Mark rolled his eyes. "I thought we came here for the hayride, family."

"Oh, hush, Marcus. Let your little brother have his moment like you had yours."

"That young man will never forget what you did for him back there, son," Mr. Driarson said. "I'm very proud of you for that, King. But you're going to have to tell me more about how you've been embarrassing your mother."

"There's nothing to discuss, dear. No harm, no foul."

"I see," Mr. Driarson said, letting it go. "Well, Marcus, have you gotten everyone's hayride ticket?"

"Whoaaa," Mark replied, dodging his father's request. "I've got Regina's ticket."

"Give the boy some money, dear," Monte's mother pushed.

"See how they do me, young lady?" Mr. Driarson said, acknowledging Regina.

"Hi, Mr. and Mrs. Driarson. It's a pleasure to meet you two," Regina said as she reached out to shake their hands — Mrs. Driarson's first.

"Well, hello!" Monte and Mark's mother said with a hint of exaggeration. "It is a pleasure to finally meet you. I've heard so much about you from both boys, and it's nice to finally put a face to the stories they tell."

"Good stories, I hope," Regina replied, smiling to mask her fear of what Marcus may have told his mom. "I'm really excited for the hayride. I've never been on one, and Marcus has been saying how it's a family tradition for you all."

"We've been going on the hayride together since Mark attended Three Pyramids Elementary School," Mrs. Driarson said.

"Sometimes, we miss a year when it rains," Mr. Driarson added. "But for the most part, we always try to go together as a family."

As Monte's parents continued to get to know Regina, Monte spotted Nathalie in the distance. She was standing next to Lizbeth at the cotton candy booth half-listening — and staring back at Monte.

"Hi," Monte mouthed and awkwardly waved quickly.

"Hi," she replied, doing the same.

Slipping away from his family, Monte made the walk to Nathalie to take advantage of the moment.

This is it, he thought. *If I just own it and apologize, she'll go on the hayride with me.*

Monte took in a deep breath as his heart raced. He picked up his feet carefully to avoid falling and embarrassing himself.

"Hey, you got a moment?" Monte said, reaching out to hold Nathalie's hand. "I'm sorry about earlier. What I said. What I did. How I've been acting. You were a hundred and ten percent right, and I want to thank you for sharing those hard truths with me."

"Oh, Monte," Nathalie said, turning red. "I'd expect you to do the same for me if I turned into a brat, too."

"Hey!" Monte protested.

Nathalie laughed as she pulled at one of her curls.

"So." Monte awkwardly paused, gathering himself. "We've got room for one more on our hayride wagon," he said hopefully.

"Oh, yeah?" Nathalie said, looking back at Lizbeth. "Would that seat happen to be for me, by chance?"

Monte smiled as he pulled at Nathalie's hand, still holding on. "Excuse us, Lizbeth," he said, leading Nathalie away. "I'm going to need to borrow her for a bit."

"Yo, Monte!" Mark shouted. "I've got your tickets; let's go!"

"You two get outta here," Lizbeth said. "I'll be at the dunk tank with Bao."

Nathalie, still smiling and looking at Monte, said, "How did you know I was going to say yes to the hayride?"

Monte smiled back and winked at Nathalie. "I just thought I knew you."

Inspire The Masses

ABOUT THE AUTHOR

As a former elementary teacher, Michael A. Woodward, Jr. has found himself back in the classroom as a current PhD student at Barry University in Miami, FL.

Throughout his studies, he has collected a Bachelor's degree in Business Administration from Florida A&M University (FAMU) and a Masters degree in Education from the University of Nevada, Las Vegas (UNLV). He is inspired daily by his three sons and fiancée, whom he credits for his entire source of motivation.

However, a huge part of Michael's inspiration comes from the stories he carries of being in the classroom surrounded by black and brown scholars who struggled to find fiction literature that they could see themselves in. More often than not, a feeling of disconnect overcame his students during class-wide trips to the library between them and the books they lifted from its shelves.

As such, Woodward fought through his personal self-doubt and disbelief in his ability to write in an attempt to create a story that is symbolic to the hundreds of thousands of children who stem from low-income communities and face inequities that many adults may never have to encounter.

One day, he believes, all children will have the opportunity to take advantage of a deserving and equitable education, and it's his belief that it begins with us as their educators.

ACKNOWLEDGMENTS

While I find the majority of my strength from the Lord, much of it comes from the company I keep. I know that it is through my village of friends and family I find my greatest seeds of confidence.

From casual conversations with siblings about the neighborhood bully of a dog to being bitten by one as a child and it haunting me for the remainder of my life, I thank everyone that has inspired me to share our stories to the generations to follow. I thank my family for pouring their strength into me to push through.

Can you believe that it's been 8 books in 18 months? I certainly can't, yet I know few people who can believe it and those are my mothers. Thank you, ladies – not only for your unyielding love and support, but more importantly for your belief in me.

To the remainder of my immediate family inclusive of my father and fiancée – thank you. Thank you for your patience and endless words of affirmations.

"I can do all things through Christ who strengthens me." Philippians 4:13 NKJV.

Inspire the Masses

Michael A. Woodward, Jr.

CPSIA information can be obtained
at www.ICGtesting.com
Printed in the USA
LVHW092117020721
691787LV00006B/134/J

9 781087 956336